UNDERSTANDING MISS UNDERSTANDING

*A RIVERVIEW ANIMAL SHELTER
MYSTERY NOVEL*

HELEN A. BEMIS

outskirts
press

Outskirts Press, Inc.
http://www.outskirtspress.com

ISBN: 978-1-9772-2809-3

Cover image by Mechelle Roskiewicz

Outskirts Press and the "OP" logo are trademarks belonging to Outskirts Press, Inc.

PRINTED IN THE UNITED STATES OF AMERICA

Praise for *Understanding Sassie*,
for *Understanding Sassie II,*
and for *Understanding Champ*

I so enjoyed returning to the characters I first met in *Understanding Sassie.* I like reading a continuing story about familiar characters while being introduced to new information. *Sassie II* does both. The widening circle of people and animals that are inter-related help carry the narrative through plausible problems. This story demonstrates how the human family/community works together to solve problems, while giving new insights into how animals work together to help each other as well. I'm thrilled to know a third book is forthcoming. The building of this peaceful place reminds me of Jan Karon's "Mitford" series. I look forward to learning where Sassy takes me and what Sassy has to teach me next!

Jane Stratton, Registered Nurse

Understanding Sassie II is a wonderful and heartwarming story that brings about lots of different emotions. While reading about the lives of the various characters and their connections with each other and with the dogs in the book, I found it to be suspenseful, happy, sad, fun, and an especially great love story. Enjoyed it immensely!

Nancy Pic, Dental Hygienist

CONTENTS

DEDICATION

To all the working dogs.

ACKNOWLEDGMENTS

To my beloved husband, Bruce: A special "thank you" to you for your patience, encouragement, and understanding during the writing of this book.

To Doug Cooper: You may hold the title of "coach," but you have become so much more. You're my teacher, my punctuation specialist, and a special friend. I've often said that you are worth your weight in gold. Actually, you are worth more than that to me. Your wisdom and "fine-tuning" of my writing have been, for me, invaluable!

To Mechelle: Thank you for sharing your art. My covers are special because of your talent in drawing awesome dogs. It is an honor to be able to use these pictures.

To you, the reader: A special thank you. I am grateful for your kind words, and I have been delighted to hear from you how much dog-wisdom you have discovered within each of my stories.

PREFACE

Why do some of us persistently seek to understand?

The American College Dictionary defines "understanding" as follows: "The quality or condition of one who understands: comprehension."

In this book, you will meet someone who seeks to understand almost everything. I can identify with her because I'm also one who seeks to understand. To me knowledge supports wisdom, and I love to share wisdom with others.

Whether I share a funny joke or an amazing story, I love to see others smile and enjoy life more fully.

May this story also bring understanding AND joy to your day,

—*Helen*

FOREWORD

Are puppies being poisoned at the Riverview Animal Shelter? If so, by whom? And why?

That mystery develops in this sixth book of Helen A. Bemis's Riverview series:

Understanding Sassie
Understanding Sassie, II
Understanding Champ
Understanding Trixie
Understanding Tippie
Understanding Miss Understanding

Each book can be read on its own, but many readers will enjoy having familiar characters reappear in new situations, emphasizing relationships among people, among animals, and the interactions between the species.

In *Understanding Miss Understanding,* we find young adults Alice and Ben serving as counselors at the Kids' Camp run over the summer at the Riverview Animal Shelter by Jane, Ruth, and Millie to teach local youth how to care for and train their dogs.

Seriously sick dogs and an ill camper make Alice into an amateur detective, aiding a real detective, James, from the local police force to seek the truth of the apparent poisonings. Her dog, Misty, plays a role in solving the puzzle.

Alice's inquisitiveness and insights earn her the playful nickname, "Miss Understanding."

The results of the investigation put Alice on a new course for her life, one that intersects with the path being taken by Tippie's owner, Art, on his way to becoming a veterinarian.

Another camper's life changes greatly, too.

It is my continuing pleasure to work as coach and editor for Helen A. Bemis, a dog training professional and now an author, who writes even when it hurts and demonstrates my favorite definition of "class," "grace under pressure."

Douglas Winslow Cooper, PhD
WriteYourBookWithMe.com
May 2020

1

THE BLACKOUT

Riverview Animal Shelter's Kids' Camp was noisy. Tonight, it was also very dark.

Was it wise for me to have gone outside? Alice asked herself. Thunder reminded her of possible nearby danger.

A lightning strike had already created a blackout at the camp. Her flashlight was the only light visible in the pouring rain.

I've always loved these Riverview Animal Shelter summer camps. However, what I never liked were the violent summer rainstorms. Roaring down the mountain, they always gave a surprise attack. These storms are nothing like the gentle rainstorms I'd experience back home.

Alice thought about her close friend Art, and she felt sad. Art had not come to camp this year. He had told her he had a chance to do an internship with an award-winning professor, and he wanted to spend the summer at the college.

I asked him to please write to me during this time, she thought. *Maybe that was an unrealistic request. I know that when he becomes excited about his schoolwork, he rarely calls and almost never writes. I DO miss his company!*

One of the shelter's Kids' Camps now featured one week

of round-the-clock camping. Full-time was a bigger responsibility for the Riverview Animal Shelter personnel, but they felt it was a worthwhile experience for the students.

Each student was required to bring a crate for his or her dog. The dogs' crates would be located in the cabins at night and outside the cabins during the daytime dog-resting times.

Alice gazed at the Boys' Cabin and saw a narrow stream of light.

"WHO is there?" Alice demanded in an authoritative voice. She felt scared but hoped that her voice had not reflected that.

"Is that you, Alice?" Ben answered.

"When the lights went out, I decided that it might be wise to check on the students."

Ben was one of the twins who had come to the Riverview Animal Shelter's first Kid's Camp many years before. He had now grown to a six-foot two-inch good-looking young man.

Alice was impressed that he would be attending an eminent college in the fall on an athletic scholarship. Like many of the girls, she loved to look into his blue eyes. She would never admit to wanting to run her hands through his curly blond hair.

Alice had noticed that Ben was always well dressed. She suspected that even at this hour of the night, if she could see him, he would still be dressed handsomely.

Alice responded to Ben's answer, "I came out to check on the Girls' Cabin. Would you like to check together?"

If the truth be told, her suggestion, for Alice, was almost a necessity. She was definitely not happy about walking alone in the dark.

As she approached Ben's location, she said, "Ben, has

the Riverview Shelter ever mentioned having a Blackout Plan?"

Ben shook his head no, then said it aloud, realizing she might not have seen him shake his head.

Through their years at camp, Alice and Ben had been given more and more responsibilities. Today, they were both Senior Counselors, and as such, they were more responsible for the students.

As they approached the Boys' Cabin door, the lights came on. Both sighed in relief. Ben was the first to speak, "I do hope this means that the lights are on to stay!"

Alice said, "I understand that feeling," and added, "Let's check inside the cabin on the boys and make sure that everything is good."

They slowly opened the door. The boys were sound asleep... but that did not last very long. The campers' dogs began to bark, and soon everyone was up and wondering why "Mr. Ben" and "Miss Alice" had come into their cabin.

Apparently, the boys had gone to sleep before the power had been lost. None had realized that there had been any type of problem.

"Go back to sleep," Ben announced. He then asked Alice, "Should we check the Girls' Cabin?"

When they got to the cabin, they were happy to see that the girls had also gone to bed early. Once again, the dogs soon woke the girls, and once again, the campers were told to go back to sleep.

"I guess we worried for nothing," Alice told Ben.

"Yes, but we did take responsibility for the students, and I believe that was what we should have done."

Waving each other good-night, they retreated to their own sleeping quarters and prepared for bed.

They did not know this would be the last camp night of resting. This night's storm had ended but there would be many stormy nights ahead.

Someone had taken advantage of the blackout.

2

WHAT HAPPENED TO CLYDE?

Yes, indeed, someone took advantage of the blackout. That someone believed that he had the solution to creating a super-dog.

He had been studying the use of chemicals and was convinced that he had discovered a secret formula for greatly enhancing a dog's abilities. The blackout was the perfect cover for what he had to do. *I will start with a very young dog,* he thought.

The morning after the blackout, the weather was sunny and the sky provided a delightful pattern of fluffy clouds. The wind caressed the camp with gentle and refreshing breezes.

Alice woke up on her own, just before her alarm was about to ring. She was rested and ready to start her day of counselor responsibilities. *I need to talk to Jane before the staff meeting*, she thought. She quickly showered and dressed. *Last night's blackout did not create an emergency, but I still think there should have been a plan for this type of occurrence. I'd like to have an idea of possible action during a storm like that one.*

Alice would soon discover the truth about the prior night's blackout.

Jane was in her office preparing notes for the upcoming staff meeting. She was now a semi-retired Supervisor of the Riverview Animal Shelter. Millie and Ruth, who had been her head dog trainers, were now called the joint CEOs of the shelter. They claimed that the initials stood for "Chief Encouragement Officers."

Jane looked up when she heard someone running into the building.

Alice, too, had seen a person running, and when she saw him heading toward the front door, her destination as well, she let him enter first.

Jane recognized the young man as the person that Fred, her sheep-farming friend, had hired to help him work on the sheep farm. Fred had reduced the number of his sheep that now lived on the farm, but he still needed a full-time helper to do the heavy work.

The young man stopped in front of Jane's desk, trying urgently to say something. However, breathless, he could only say a word or two.

"Sick! The vet! Come!" With hand-signals and an expression of panic, he let Jane know something serious had happened.

Jane asked him, "Is it Fred?"

The young man shook his head, no.

Then Jane asked, "Is it Ann, Fred's wife?" Again, the young man shook his head, no.

Thinking *what should I now ask?* she questioned, "Is it one of the sheep?" The young man again shook his head, no.

By this time, the young man was finally able to say, "It's one of the Border Collies, Daisy's pup, Clyde."

Alice had followed the young man into Jane's office. When she overheard the news, she exclaimed, "That's my dog, Misty's brother. What happened?"

Jane remembered that last year she had given two of Daisy's puppies to Fred and Ann, a special gift for their wedding anniversary. Fred had promptly called the female "Bonnie" and the male "Clyde."

The staff had already rushed Clyde to the local veterinarian's office.

They had dropped off the young man so he could tell Jane the news. When he finally was able to speak normally, he reported to Jane that Ann had noticed that Clyde had been trying to vomit; because his stomach was not distended, Ann did not suspect that Clyde had the bloat. However, Jane did feel that something was seriously wrong.

Jane questioned the young man to discover to which vet Clyde had been taken. Then she immediately called this veterinarian to see if she could talk to someone about Clyde.

The receptionist responded politely that she could only tell Jane that the veterinarian was in with this patient; she added that as soon as it was possible for him to do so, she would have him call her.

Jane realized it was time for the staff meeting, but she hesitated.

Millie, nearby, understood that Jane was preparing to go to the staff meeting. Millie had heard most of the conversation and knew Jane would want to be by the phone when the call came in about Clyde. She realized that Jane would also want to be at the staff meeting.

"You could stay here," Millie told Jane. "I know you have made some notes for the meeting. I'll use your notes to run the meeting, and I can send a runner back to you if there are any questions."

Relieved, Jane sat back down. She appreciated the support and comfort of her chair and her staff.

Millie turned to Alice and said, "Please join me. I think most of the staff is already in the meeting room."

Jane watched them go into the meeting room. She wondered, *what could have happened to Clyde? It was just yesterday that Ann was telling me that he looked to be the picture of health.*

3

ONLY A RUMOR?

Millie and Alice walked into the Large Group Instruction Room, usually used during the major camp functions, big enough to accommodate a large number of people.

The tables and chairs could be easily re-arranged for almost any situation. Demonstrations were easily seen and the sound system conveniently adjusted for large or small crowds.

Today it had been set up for the smaller use of a staff meeting. Alice had noticed Ben was pointing to her and then to the seat next to him, so she came over and sat by him. He leaned over and asked, "Did you get a chance to talk to Jane about the blackout?"

She shook her head no and then added, "Shh, the meeting's about to start. We'll talk later."

Standing in front of the group, Millie began, "Welcome to the second full day of camp. Last night's storm was noisy, but it seems many, if not all, of our campers slept through the power outage and blackout we experienced.

"According to all the storm-event reports I've received; it seemed a problem-free night. Thank you, all, for your vigilance and responsible work during this situation.

"The grounds are soaked, and we fear it could become very muddy if we try to work on these areas today. Plan to use the smaller paved area for our outdoor training to-day. It's a back-up parking lot, but no one is scheduled to be parked there.

"Please understand that there will be no shade in this area, so keep in mind the risk of heat exhaustion. Continue to encourage drinking water. We all need to keep hydrated. Also remember that the shelter is air-conditioned and avail-able, if needed, for a break from the sun.

"The weather forecast for today is for sunny skies but cooler temperatures. I noticed a mild breeze as I came into camp this morning. That should help keep the outdoor tem-peratures at a comfortable level.

"Before we dismiss for breakfast, are there any ques-tions?" No one asked a question. Millie dismissed the group by saying, "You are free to go. Enjoy your breakfast."

When Millie returned to Jane's office, she saw Jane had her purse in her hand and looked anxious to leave.

Jane saw Millie's puzzled look and said, "Let Ruth know that I will be going to the vet's office to see Clyde. I can't en-dure it any longer, just sitting here and waiting for a phone call."

"I understand," Millie replied. "Please be careful. I know you want to race to see Clyde, but you could get hurt if you hurry, and that will not help this situation."

Jane quickly realized the wisdom of Millie's advice. "I promise. I will be careful. I'll even try to travel less than the speed limit!" Jane smiled when she said this. Millie knew Jane understood Millie was concerned for her friend.

Although Jane was worried about the puppy, she did make a point to follow all the traffic rules, especially making sure to travel at a moderate speed, not her habit.

Reaching the veterinarian's office, she parked and then ran into the building.

Ann and Fred were in the waiting room. With her arms outstretched, Jane gave Ann and then Fred big hugs. Fred was unusually somber and made no attempt to tease Jane, a definite sign he was worried about Clyde.

All three turned when they heard the examination room door open.

Seeing the questioning look on their faces, the vet said, "I believe that Clyde went into an anaphylactic shock. This is a severe reaction to exposure to something Clyde is allergic to, like a bee sting or peanuts. Has Clyde ever shown that he has had any allergies?"

When Ann and Fred shook their heads, the doctor continued by explaining his treatment for Clyde. "I have given him some medication to reverse the allergic reaction, but I'll need to run a number of blood tests to see if I can determine the exact cause of his problem.

"I won't lie to you. He is one very sick dog. I have administered an IV to help keep him stable. I will want to watch him closely. He is struggling, but he is a strong-willed dog. The next 24 hours will determine if he'll survive.

"Some of his symptoms are unusual. I'm going to check with a number of specialists and see if any of them can help me shine a light on this mystery. I'm hoping the blood work will expose the cause of his sudden illness.

"I'd like you to go in and talk to him. I believe that your voices will help him to relax. Remember to try to sound happy. He needs to hear your love, not your concern."

They nodded in assent, and as Fred and Ann started to walk into the examination room, Jane said to Fred, "Maybe next time Ann should bring some chocolate chip cookies for a get-well present." That brought a small, wry smile to

Fred's face, who knew that Jane meant well but she did not realize that chocolate is often toxic for dogs.

Meanwhile, at camp, Alice began to hear a disturbing rumor: "Did you know that a dog had been poisoned during the black-out?"

At first, Alice felt that someone was attempting to scare the other campers. As she thought about the comments, she began to wonder if someone had been referring to Clyde.

"Is that rumor true?" One of the campers asked her.

She reassured that camper that it had only been a rumor, but when another camper asked her, "Is my dog in danger of being poisoned?" she began to feel that someone needed to find the source of this rumor.

⸻⸺«◉»⸺⸻

I should not have injected that young dog in the dark! He thought. He was unhappy that his targeted dog had gotten so sick. *I must have read the dose wrong. I measured the chemicals in the hypodermic syringe, but now I wonder if I gave the dog too large a dose. I'll be more careful next time. Maybe I'll use one of the feisty rescue dogs. Can an older dog tolerate these chemicals a little better?*

4

THE FOURTH DAY OF CAMP

On the fourth day of camp, Jane came to the shelter early, as she often did. However, instead of going straight to her office, she decided to look in on the shelter animals.

Maybe I feel this way because I received good news about Clyde, she thought. *They are still keeping him lightly sedated, but Clyde is responding with a tail wag whenever Ann and Fred come to visit. He is going to live!*

As Jane opened the door to the shelter's cat section, she was pleased to see that most of the cats were resting quietly.

When she moved to the shelter's dog section, it was a different story. She had immediately heard the sound of a dog attempting to vomit. She phoned Katherine, the shelter vet, when she located the sick dog.

Katherine had just woken up and was thinking of rolling over for a few more minutes of sleep when her phone rang.

"No, I was awake," she said. She listened to Jane, then interrupted her, saying, "I'll be right over!"

The phone call had awakened her husband, Donald, who asked, "What's up?"

In a hurried reply, Jane answered, "It was Jane. She's worried and thinks one of the shelter dogs is displaying the same symptoms as Clyde did. I'm going to the shelter."

When Katherine saw the shelter dog, she had Jane help her move the dog to her car to transport this dog immediately to her office for treatment. This dog needed to be stabilized immediately. Clearly, he was suffering a dangerous allergic reaction.

Jane watched Katherine leave and decided, *it is time to call the police!*

"It does seem suspicious," the policeman was telling Jane. "I'd like to have one of our detectives look at this situation. It could be a coincidence, but I think it may indicate a crime."

Jane agreed to his suggestion of a detective's examination, and the officer turned to leave. "One of our detectives will be contacting you."

Millie walked in, just in time to hear the officer's last statement. She looked at Jane and asked, "What's up? Are you all right?"

Meanwhile, Alice had also been getting up early, joining Millie and Jane for morning coffee. She was enjoying their morning ritual of "girl time." She too heard the police officer's comment and Millie's question. She asked Jane, "Are you alright?"

Jane began to explain. "I had decided to look in at the animals this morning...."

As Jane concluded her story, Millie and Alice both became alarmed. Jane remarked, "I'm glad they will be sending over a detective, but I sincerely hope this is not a criminal matter!"

At Katherine's veterinary office, she made sure several blood samples were drawn. *I'm going to call Clyde's veterinarian and see if he found anything suspicious*, she decided. *I'd like to compare our chemical analysis and see what could be contributing to this severe allergy reaction. Once again, a dog's life may have been saved by our quick intervention.*

———»«◉»«———

The afternoon of the fourth day, a very different set of thoughts were going through the mind of a very different person at the shelter: *I've got to check over my chemical formula once again. Why are my dogs getting a severe allergic reaction to my chemical mixture? I've done the research. What am I missing? I know I have the answer to a "Super Dog," and it should be working. Maybe if I add another chemical that will counteract the allergy trigger? I may go back and work with another puppy.*

He would try once again.

5

A MIXED DAY AT RIVERVIEW

Alice always enjoyed her camp experiences.
However, as she watched the work being done at
the Riverview Shelter, she decided to become one
of the needed volunteers as well.

Many of the dogs needed to be walked. Alice often volunteered for this duty whenever she had time free from camp duties. Other dogs had more pressing needs.

Her heart went out to some of the abandoned dogs brought into the shelter, such as the one that had come into the shelter late the day before, a pregnant mixed-breed that had been left tied to a telephone pole, with no food or water.

This day, she had the opportunity to work with Katherine, as the vet examined the dogs that were new arrivals. The pregnant female was one of the dogs scheduled for Katherine's examination.

While helping her, Alice bombarded Katherine with questions. "How can you tell when she will have her puppies?" Alice inquired about the pregnant female. "She looks awfully thin. Will her puppies survive? Is the dog's temperature the same as a human temperature? How can you stay so positive and happy when you see the abuse of some of these animals? I don't know if I could handle the responsibilities of becoming a veterinarian. I admire Art for his attempt to follow in your footsteps."

Katherine enjoyed her son's – Art's – camper friend. Even though Katherine was sad that he had not come home for the summer, she understood the love he had for his college work. Katherine welcomed Alice's company. She certainly was interested in everything at the shelter!

Katherine looked at the pregnant female and replied to Alice's questions about this dog.

"The dog's body is actually what tells me when she is ready to give birth to her puppies."

"Okay, I can understand that," Alice replied.

Katherine continued, "It looks like they may arrive soon. We have given her extra nourishment so that her puppies should arrive in good condition. I'll be back tonight to check on this gal. If you get a chance, come and join me. I have a feeling that tonight will see the arrival of her litter."

This was one more bit of excitement for Alice. She had begun to research the symptoms of anaphylaxis shock. She found a fascination with the puzzle pieces of knowledge in relation to the many topics she had researched. *I'm really beginning to feel satisfaction in solving mysteries by research,* she thought.

At camp, they had been working on an obedience trial workout. It was a repetitious, but needed, discipline for the dogs. Many of the campers wanted to compete. A few of the dogs had actually begun to earn a "leg" or two in AKC competition.

In the official AKC competition, a dog needed three legs to receive a title. Each leg consisted of gaining at least the minimum number of points, along with no disqualifications toward the leg of each title. Besides, the leg was mandated to be judged by a judge that had not officiated at any of the other legs for that dog.

Ben had joined Alice on the practice field. "What do you think we should practice as our first exercise today?" Ben asked.

"Let's get them moving first and then practice a few sit-stays," Alice answered. Then she added, "What exercises from yesterday do you think need more work today?"

As they talked, they began to plan the schedule for the campers. They balanced the nearly stationary events with the more active ones, and sometimes the dogs needed more active time to tire them enough so they could relax when needed.

The camp kitchen had received snack donations for the students. These included a large number of the small bags of chips, some bags of peanut M&M's, several small packages of cheese crackers, and a few bags of popcorn.

They decided to hand out the chips that day, the cheese crackers that night, and maybe the M&M's during the next day's lunch.

After the productive camp day and after their suppers, most of the campers retired to their cabins.

Alice was excited about the possible birth of puppies. *I hope that Katherine is correct and puppies will be born tonight.* She hurried to the shelter and saw Donald working in the cat area.

"Hi, Mr. Donald," Alice greeted him, and then she asked, "has Miss Katherine arrived at the shelter?"

He shook his head no and then said, "We did get a letter from Art today. Would you like to read it?"

Knowing the answer, Donald did not wait, and he handed the letter to her. She practically danced as she reached for the letter. She quickly scanned the letter and then re-read it slowly. Art wrote that he was excited to work with this professor. He described in detail the work that they had been doing, but Alice did not understand many of the big, technical words. She smiled when she read that he was ex-cited and happy. He also mentioned that he missed every-one and named some of them particularly.

"He said he missed me!" Alice exclaimed when she saw her name mentioned.

After returning the letter to Donald, she thought about how, like Art, she had been enjoying her own research. She asked Donald: "I know you've done a lot of research using the Internet; how can you separate someone's opinion from the true facts about a subject?"

"Good question," Donald said. "Through the years I have checked the Internet information with other sources and with experts who are well-known and published in the subject. I think of the Internet material as possibly true, but I have found that I like to check more than one source of information."

Alice thought for a minute and said, "I can understand the need to do that."

Just then, Katherine walked in; in an affectionate ges-ture, she messed up Alice's already tousled hair. Smiling, Alice said, "Hi, Miss Katherine. Why did you mess up my gorgeously styled hair?" It was a running joked she shared with her friend and mentor.

This made Katherine smile. As she approached Donald, she gave him a kiss hello.

"Any news to report?" Katherine asked.

When Donald indicated there was none, Katherine peeked into Jane's office.

Jane had no new news to report either.

A quiet day, it seemed.

To check on the pregnant mom, Katherine moved to the dog section of the shelter. She found Alice there, petting the momma dog.

When she looked up and saw Katherine, Alice commented, "She seems to be breathing hard."

Katherine knelt beside Alice and examined the dog. "Yes, I think her time is near. Could you tell Donald and Jane that we will be staying here tonight? I'd like to make sure she is as comfortable as possible."

Early the next morning, the puppies were born. The female was an attentive mother but extremely tired. Katherine and Alice were tired, too.

"Let's go get some rest," Katherine told Alice. "Our mother should be fine, for now. We'll check her later this morning. She needs her rest, and the puppies are content as they nestle beside her. All is well."

Katherine and Alice did leave the puppies and their mother, but all would NOT be well.

6

TIME TO CALL THE POLICE

After leaving the new mother and her puppies, Katherine had posted a note on Jane's office door. Jane usually came to the shelter early, so she figured this would be the best method of reporting the birth of the puppies to Jane. After all, at this time of the morning, everyone would be sound asleep.

Were they ALL asleep? No.

He slowly opened the door to the dog section of the shelter. *Is the rumor true?* He wondered. He needed to check for himself. *Had a litter of puppies been born during the night?*

The puppies' mother heard someone approaching her area. She gave a "stay-away" growl. If someone was coming in her direction, she wanted them to know that they were not welcome anywhere near her puppies.

He came prepared. He figured that the female dog might want to protect her puppies. He had brought a strip of steak and had made sure that he had laced it with a strong sedative for dogs. As he hoped, she ate some of the steak and fell right asleep.

Holding one of the puppies, he smiled. He placed the

needle of the syringe between the tiny toes of the puppy and administered his newest chemical mixture. *Now there should be success.*

When Jane arrived, she went straight to her office. She found Katherine's puppy birth-announcement note on her door and read it. *How nice! I'll take a peek at this newest dog family.*

At first, when she looked at the new mom and her puppies, she thought that they were quietly resting. Then she noticed the partially eaten steak on the floor. Taking a closer look, she saw that most of the puppies were softly nuzzling their mother, but she seemed to be unresponsive. At that point, Jane noted that one of the puppies was not moving at all.

She raced back to her office and made a phone call to Katherine.

Then she decided to call the police.

Soon after her call, a young detective arrived at the shelter, just as Millie and Alice were meeting with Jane for coffee.

"Good Morning," the detective greeted the group. "I'm Detective James Fields of the Riverview Police Department. I understand that someone seems to be poisoning the dogs in this community. There was a call to the station this morning concerning a possible poisoning here in the shelter. Could you direct me to this location?"

James was a man in his mid-twenties, tall, with an athletic build. His hair was jet black and his eyes appeared to hide a secret joke that only he was aware of. Alice was already impressed with this policeman.

Alice followed James and Jane as they walked back to the Riverview shelter's dog section. Alice stopped at the door's entrance, unsure whether she wanted to enter the area and see the details of this bad situation.

The detective stood outside the enclosure that held the dog family; he had been told that no one had been allowed into the enclosure, and he decided to call his police station.

He connected to the Forensic Science Lab. With a quick explanation of the situation, he requested an investigation of this so-far-undisturbed crime area.

"The team will be here soon," he told Jane. "Please don't let anyone enter this enclosure until the team has completed their work here.

"You were wise not to enter this enclosure. That fact should help us to get some evidence that may help us catch this person."

Alice was still in the hall outside the dog section when James came through its door, ready to report back to the police station.

Alice stopped the detective and asked, "When you spoke to Jane, I overheard you say something about a Crime Scene Investigation unit. What exactly is it that they do?"

James took a second look at this pretty girl. He did notice her when he first met the group in Jane's office, but then he had concentrated on his job instead of engaging her in a conversation. She seemed sincerely interested in understanding the job of a Crime Scene Investigator; however, he needed to get back to the police station. *I wonder if she would be willing to see me later. If she accepts a coffee meeting, maybe I'll get a chance to know her.*

His immediate answer to Alice was both truthful and hopeful, "I'm sorry I don't have time now to explain, but could we meet for coffee later at the Riverview Hospital cafeteria? I'll have time to explain more about our Crime Lab and the work it does."

Alice blushed and quickly nodded a yes, but then asked, "Why the Riverview Hospital?" James replied, "It may sound strange to say this, but I have discovered that this coffee shop has been, for me, the most enjoyable and relaxing location for having a cup of coffee."

Alice smiled and said, "I can understand wanting to have coffee at an enjoyable and relaxing location."

They then agreed on 7:00 p.m. for their coffee meeting.

At the Riverview Animal Shelter, rumors had been flying all day. Someone had seen the police vehicle parked that morning in front of the shelter. That's when a camper announced, "I know that another dog has been poisoned!"

Everyone was talking at the camp's evening meal about the dog poisoning rumor. No one seemed to pay much attention to the food. Perhaps they were a little wary of it. The desert was the choice of cookies or the donated bags of M&M chocolate-covered peanut treats. Some of the campers ate the cookies and also put a package of the candy into their pockets.

Later that evening, the appearance of a hospital ambulance near one of the cabins caused a lot of alarm.

"What happened?" Ben asked Alice.

She shook her head as if to say, "I don't know."

The description of the camp's emergency began to be shared. Many of the campers saw a similarity between this human victim and the poisoned dogs. Was someone poisoning humans as well?

Is anyone, animal or human, safe at this Riverview Animal Shelter?

Alice became determined to ask Detective Fields about this disturbing situation. *I'll be sure to ask him when we meet for coffee.*

The coffee meeting would take place at Riverview Hospital. Both Alice and Detective Fields sought answers to this escalating problem before more harm was done.

7

COMPLETE CAMP CLEAN-UP

Alice wanted to visit the injured camper before meeting Officer Fields for their coffee meeting.

The student was still in the ICU, the Intensive Care Unit of the hospital. Alice had not realized that she would not be allowed to enter the patient's room, the rule for ICU patient visits was "family only."

When Jane had come to the hospital, she had come at a time when the family had been in the room. When they realized that Jane was the Supervisor of the Riverview Animal Shelter and that she was at the hospital, they wanted to speak with her. They had moved to the waiting room to talk.

Jane noticed Alice enter the ICU area and motioned to her to join them in the waiting room. She then introduced Alice to the hospitalized camper's family.

Jane told Alice, "The family tells me that their son did have a peanut allergy, but that it had been a mild reaction up until now. They never reported it to us because they had never felt that it had been a real problem."

Some allergies get more severe as one grows older. This was a "wake-up" call for the family. The doctor said that the camper was fortunate that he made it on time to the hospital emergency room. "The anaphylaxis allergic reaction that he had this time was life-threatening. He will need to carry an epinephrine autoinjector with him at all times and he must be aware in the future of any product that contains peanuts."

Realizing there might be other hazards at the camp, Jane had decided to shut down the camp for a couple of weeks. The student campers would be able to return after the complete clean-up and would receive an extra free week of camp to make up for the shut-down. *I will feel better if we make sure there are no other possible allergy problems within the camp.*

Alice was relieved to hear that this hospitalization was only allergy-related, and she also wanted to be a part of the clean-up work.

"Can I stay during the shut-down to help with the clean-up?" Alice asked Jane. "I believe I might be able to stay with Miss Katherine and Mr. Donald during that time."

Jane smiled at Alice, saying, "We'll talk about the shut-down details when we get back to the shelter."

Alice checked the time, and she saw that she was due to meet with Detective Fields in the hospital coffee shop. She got up to leave, after expressing get-well wishes for the camper.

As she walked into the hospital coffee shop, she could feel a homey feeling in the area. The nearest waitress was smiling as she filled the partially empty coffee cups. The arrangement of tables and chairs gave some privacy but still looked comfortable and inviting. *Now I can understand why James enjoys having coffee here*, Alice thought.

She then saw that Detective Fields had already been seated and was relaxing with his cup of steaming hot coffee. She noticed that he had changed from his uniform into a blue polo shirt that appeared to match the color of his eyes. When he saw Jane, he signaled to her to join him and then got up to greet her. That was when she noticed that he was also wearing a pair of old blue jeans.

After ordering coffee from the waitress, Alice began to speak. "Officer Fields...."

So did the detective, "Have you heard...?"

"Me first!" Alice insisted.

Laughing, James replied, "Only if you call me 'James.' I refuse to be 'Officer Fields' when I'm off duty and having coffee."

"Okay," Alice agreed, "I just spoke to the parents of the hospitalized camper. He was not poisoned by anyone! The camper has a peanut allergy and had eaten some M&M chocolate-covered peanuts."

"Guess we better not share this information with the news media or say that M&M candy was responsible for this emergency problem," James replied. "It could be a bad advertisement for M&M's business. On the other hand," he added, "it might be a good reminder to those who have such peanut allergies."

Alice liked his way of looking at things, and she decided to ask about something that puzzled her, "Why do you wish to be called 'James' instead of 'Jim'?"

James felt comfortable with Alice. He appreciated that she liked to ask questions and had a love of learning. He could tell that she honestly wanted to understand the answers to her many questions, so he began to explain, "My mom's name was 'Kristine.' She hated to have anyone call her 'Kristie.'" She threatened everyone, when she named me James, that she had wanted me to be called "James" and that NO one would be allowed to nickname me, 'Jim.'

"I liked that this made me feel special. I believe that I am using the name James to honor my mother."

It occurred to Alice that she would not want the nickname "Al," and she said so.

Alice almost asked if his mom had died, but she saw the look on his face and noticed his silence; she decided to sip on her coffee.

James was quiet and thoughtful for a minute and then changed the subject. "I believe you wanted to know more information about the term 'Crime Scene Investigator.'"

He offered an explanation of the CSI field. "I've often admired how CSI can work their magic to solve a crime. Today, with the ability to use DNA and other chemical and biological knowledge, they can learn amazing things from the evidence they collect at a crime location. Who did it? It is much easier to solve a crime with their help. I never was very good at science, but I do enjoy talking about what they do."

Alice told James, "Wow! I did not know that such a job existed. What are the qualifications for work in this field?"

James felt that he needed to repeat his modest appraisal of his abilities in science and then gave Alice a list of qualifications: "Sometimes, this field will only require a high school degree, but due to the competitiveness of this job field, it is recommended that a person have a bachelor's degree in forensic science, biology, natural science, or chemistry. Those that have a four-year degree in these fields will have more opportunities, however, for this work.

"Some of the work that they are responsible for are in the areas of processing crime scenes for evidence, photographing crime scenes, package labeling and transporting evidence, documenting autopsies, writing reports, testifying in court or briefing investigators, like me."

Impressed, and thinking about the sick puppy, Alice asked, "Have they found any clues at the shelter?"

James smiled and said, "Sorry, I'm not free to talk about an ongoing investigation. But I can say, it is too early for any information at this point. I'd add some advice for anyone looking for information. Keep your eyes and ears open. You may be surprised how a tiny fact can lead to an arrest of the one involved in a crime."

They both had been enjoying their conversation. Simultaneously, they did notice that the time had been getting late. Alice wasn't sure if she would be too forward if she asked for them to meet again. She need not have wondered because James had decided that he would help Alice learn more about forensic science technical work.

"Would you like a tour of our Forensic Lab?" He asked Alice.

"Would I? You bet I would!" She said, then decided she would be more lady-like if she stopped jumping around.

Laughing, James told her he would check into this possibility and let her know the details.

The next day, they announced that the camp would be closed for a major clean-up campaign. By the end of the day, all the campers had left for home. The Riverview Animal Shelter tomorrow morning would begin their plans for the big clean-up.

As Alice expected, Katherine and Donald were happy to have Alice stay with them; they knew Jane would appreciate her extra set of hands. Bright and observant, Alice might even help solve the mystery of the sick dog.

8

KATHERINE, ALICE, AND "THE CHEMIST"

Katherine was depressed. She had seen two of the shelter animals poisoned. *I thought we had rescued these animals. I wanted to believe we keep them safe until they could go to their forever homes! Instead, we have provided two animals for someone to poison.*

Usually, Katherine felt pride in her work at the Riverview Animal Shelter. They had rescued some animals that had been badly abused, and she personally had provided healing comfort for a few of these poor creatures that had suffered. *I feel helpless seeing this poisoning happen to the dogs in our care!*

Katherine had obtained the chemical analysis of the poison found in the bloodstreams of the two shelter dogs. She had asked the veterinarian who treated Clyde if he'd also had obtained a chemical analysis. He promised to send a copy of that report to Katherine within the next few days.

When she inspected the mixture of chemicals, she thought that one of the chemicals seemed familiar. However, she knew she had never done much studying of the toxicity of drugs used in the treatment of dogs. *Then why would any of these chemicals be familiar to me? I'm sure this is because this group of drugs was mentioned somewhere in my college studies. I don't think it would be a good plan to go through a mountain of interactions for every chemical to try to find an answer to why someone might use these particular drugs to poison the dogs.*

Alice, on the other hand, discovered she was very interested in the chemistry of these cases. The young police detective had opened her eyes to the whole new world CSI and its work. They were using science, a fascinating concept for Alice. *I'd like to understand more about chemical side-effects*, she thought.

Katherine enjoyed sharing the chemical information with Alice. The detective on this dog poisoning case had sparked Alice's interest in forensic science nearly to a passion. Katherine enjoyed this new side of Alice. *I wonder*, Katherine thought. *Is it the subject material or the handsome detective?*

Shelter Supervisor Jane was convinced that a clean-up was the answer to the camp problem.

Alice, however, believed that the only connection between the dog and human patients was that there was a possible allergic reaction in two of the three cases.

The autopsy on the last animal victim had not indicated any occurrence of an allergic, anaphylactic shock. That cause of death was a direct result of toxic poisoning. The dog had died of heart failure due to the multiple deadly chemicals in its bloodstream.

Alice was working with Jane to help clean, disinfect, and practically sterilize, every section of the shelter and camp.

"We have had no indication or any sign of sickness, poisoning, or problems since we started this cleaning," Jane boasted.

Alice was not sure what this proved. Her main concern these days was Katherine, definitely quieter than usual.

Even Donald noticed the change in Katherine. He decided it had something to do with Art's not coming home during this summer. *She'll snap out of it.*

Alice pulled out their photo album to test Donald's theory. "Miss Katherine, I love these pictures of Art. He would always discourage my looking through these old albums. He seemed embarrassed if I looked at them. Was there ever a time when he did something that was an embarrassment to him and that he wanted no one to know about?"

Katherine was smiling as they looked at the picture album, but when Alice asked that question, she began to laugh. "Yes, there is. I will tell you about it, but it needs to be an understanding that it is our inside joke. You know, just between the two of us. Do you promise?"

Alice was so very pleased to see her Miss Katherine happy that she was ready to promise anything. "I promise."

"As a very young child, Art loved to get into everything. It was during the time that we were working with the potty-chair. It was an old wooden chair with a hole in the seat.

"I felt I needed to disinfect this chair. But Art thought it was a very interesting item to explore. He played with it often but was not the least bit interested in using it the way it was meant to be used.

"One day he decided that the chair would make a wonderful hat. The opening was too large to have this chair sit on his head but large enough to let the opening slip over his head and down to his neck, like a collar.

"However, when he tried to get the potty chair seat off his head, he found that his ears would not comply with any method of release of this potty-styled collar.

"I really should have taken a picture of this scene, but Donald would not let me. He took pity on Art's embarrassment and managed to cut the wood in such a way that the potty-chair rim broke and he was released.

"I often smile when I think of that day, but I have never told Art the real reason that I do so. Remember the code word 'chair,' and we'll keep this as our little secret. Okay?"

"I promise," Alice repeated, continuing to laugh. Alice then frowned and confronted Katherine with her concerns. "Why are you sad now? Is it because Art is not home this summer?"

Katherine liked Alice and once again was surprised at the way she asked so many questions. *She always wants to understand,* Katherine thought. "I'm sorry if my sadness has been so obvious. I'm upset about the animals at the shelter. I love them so dearly, and now they have been hurt. I believed that this shelter was a safe place for the animals, and now I'm not happy that some of them were badly hurt here while in our care!"

"Do you think we should put up some security cameras throughout the camp?" Alice asked. "It might help to keep our animals extra safe."

"A good thought, but security cameras are expensive, and there is no way we could afford that expense at this time."

Alice pondered this and realized the truth of what Katherine had said. "Is there any other way we can keep an eye on just a part of the shelter?"

"We were recently talking about Art's baby behaviors. At that time, I had decided to place a 'Nanny-cam' in Art's bedroom. He was a very active boy and sometimes he would get out of bed and get into mischief. This was a good way to watch him without scaring him, yet still go to him and make sure that he went back into his bed."

"But no one has attempted to hurt the animals in over a

week. Wait!" Alice exclaimed, "Do you think it might be one of the campers who has been hurting our animals?" Alice became alarmed at this thought. "If we do put a Nanny-cam in that area, I think it should be something that only you and I know about."

Katherine decided this was a good idea. "Let me look for ours. I know I put it away for safekeeping, but I'm not sure exactly where the 'safekeeping' location is. Give me some time to dig it out."

The second week of cleaning quickly ended, the campers due to return on Monday.

Alice was tempted to tell James about her idea, but a promise is a promise, and although she hoped the person poisoning the animals would never come back, she thought that, just maybe, this was a CSI type of idea.

"The Chemist" was at home. He had been working, once again, with his chemicals. The Chemist had spent a lot of time checking and double-checking the information on healing and special effects from certain chemicals. *Next week I'll have another chance to test my theory. I need to make sure that the next time will succeed!*

Would his next experiment produce a Super Dog...or something else?

9

THE WEEKEND BEFORE CAMPERS RETURNED

Friday night, the clean-up of the camp was complete. Monday would see the return of the campers. For now, Alice had the weekend free for her own projects.

I'll begin some research on the list of chemicals that occurred in all of the dog incidents, she thought. *And I'd like to investigate the possibility that there is another reason, other than poisoning the dogs, for someone to repeatedly use these chemicals. There appears to be no specific reason behind the choice of the dogs involved in this situation. They seem only random choices.*

I remember that Detective James suggested that sometimes one little bit of information could solve a crime. Maybe my research can help with the answers we are looking for. I know chemistry. I know biology. Have these chemicals ever been used for a good reason to help dogs? I'll categorize and analyze each drug to see if I can find some answers. I need to understand more about these chemicals.

Using her computer, Alice did discover that a number of these chemicals had been tested for use in dogs with brain damage. One drug, in particular, was originally recommended for use in the healing of traumatic brain injuries. It was later found that a few of the dogs had developed highly enhanced intelligence, but almost all of the dogs died from toxic side-effects. This drug was removed from the market, and emergency warnings were issued throughout the veterinary community.

I believe that was when Katherine was studying to become a veterinarian. I wonder if she could tell me anything about the history of this drug. Alice turned off the computer and searched for Katherine. *I want to talk to her about my research.*

Katherine found the Nanny-cam. She wanted to show it to Alice. *I wondered why it was so hard to find. I kept overlooking the device because I had forgotten that it looked like a picture frame. It was a hidden camera in a Wi-Fi photo frame. I recall it has night vision and a motion detector. It is wire-free and will record and alert me through my smartphone.*

Katherine had just walked past the front door when it flew open.

"Surprise!" Art's loud shout certainly did surprise Katherine.

She jumped and ran to Art. "Why didn't you call? I had no idea you had finished your work with that professor. You never told me there would be a chance you'd be home, even for a short time. If you weren't so tall and me so happy, I'd be spanking you right now! Gosh, how I have missed you!"

Then, she made Art jump, as she yelled, "Donald, come and look who just walked in the door!"

Donald, in the next room, had heard someone come in, yelling, "Surprise!" At first, when he thought he heard his son's voice, he believed he had just been imagining it. He too had missed seeing Art this summer. He had finally resigned himself to waiting until Thanksgiving before Art would be able to come home, and he had tried not to dwell on his disappointment.

When Katherine yelled, "Donald" and added the words, "come and look who...," he flew out to confirm the voice he heard was his son's.

Misty, Alice's dog, had received permission to stay at Donald and Katherine's home. The downstairs was full of excitement, and her canine ears picked up this long before Alice turned off the computer. Misty zipped down the stairs right after Donald gave a bear hug to his son.

Art recognized Misty. "Is Alice here?" He asked Alice's dog in surprise. "I thought she would have gone home after camp was completed last week."

Alice was standing at the head of the stairs and didn't know whether to run downstairs and hug Art or to be lady-like and slowly descend to greet him.

Art solved her dilemma by running up the stairs and giving Alice a great big bear hug of his own.

They walked down together, each smiling broadly, and then everyone began asking questions and wanting to hear everything that all the others were saying.

Katherine ordered a Friday night pizza, and the crew spent the evening talking, until Donald reminded them that it was already early Saturday morning and they should get some sleep before the sun began to shine and announce that it was time to get up for the day.

As she lay down to go to sleep, Alice's mind raced: *What will happen now that Art is home? Will he stay and help with the camp? What will he think about the mysterious dog poisonings?*

10

MISTY

Misty was a grey-and-white female Border Collie, the perfect dog for Alice.

Although the runt of her litter, Misty had the intelligence of the Border Collie, but she did not feel compelled always to be doing something. She lacked the nervous energy of most of that breed. She was content to watch and learn by observation, rather than doing work. She felt she did not need a job. One could say that she was a lot like Alice, enjoying learning and observing, and quite content just to be with the people she loved.

As a young puppy, Misty enjoyed playing, chasing leaves in the fall and scaring the chipmunks and squirrels year-round. For Misty, pursuing these animals was a game rather than the catching of prey. She would have been as willing to let them chase her if they had wanted to do so.

Misty adored Alice and was often described as Alice's shadow. Her favorite resting spot was right beside Alice. She slept in Alice's bed, loved to be in the same room as Alice, and whenever Alice was on the computer or working on her schoolwork, Misty's head could be found by Alice's feet, under Alice's desk.

Misty was now about one year old. Alice did note how much Misty's character was similar to her own. Misty, too, wanted to learn. She observed everything around her and never seemed to miss the details. Alice enjoyed doing this as well.

Alice preferred to be with her friends and loved ones but could accept that sometimes they were not close by. Misty preferred to be with Alice but could relax near something carrying the scent of Alice. She loved to relax on Alice's bed or snuggle with one of her slippers. She would retreat, if Alice was not home, to an area having Alice's scent. There she would relax and dream of Alice. She knew how to be content with the moment.

In short, Misty loved Alice; Alice loved Misty.

Misty had recognized Art upon his return, and she was delighted to see how happy Alice had been to see him.

On Saturday night, long after Donald and Katherine left to get some sleep, Alice and Art continued to talk.

"So, what you are saying is that CSI is now your passion?" Art inquired as Alice continued to talk on and on about her newfound favorite subject. "The way you describe this work sounds interesting, and I think it is the perfect work for your personality."

"What exactly do you mean?" Alice both challenged and teased as she questioned Art. "What kind of personality do you think I have?"

Having known Alice almost forever, Art also knew when to be careful with his descriptions of this sensitive woman. "You see," he began, "forensic science is a job of puzzle-solving and lots of research. You have always enjoyed a challenge. You are competitive, and that is something that would be needed in this line of work. Accomplishment, using your brain to get a successful outcome, has always been enjoyable for you. You like to understand everything. No wonder you are nicknamed 'Miss Understanding.'"

"Yes, true. Art, these recent poisonings have been both disturbing and, for me, interesting. Thanks to Detective James, the world of CSI has become a whole new adventure for me."

The mention of James, and the light that seemed to appear in Alice's eyes whenever she said his name, irritated Art. Something about this detective was bothering Art. *Could it be that I am jealous? I've believed that I was the only special guy in Alice's life. Just because this James is a detective and has been nice to my girl is no reason for her to keep telling me complimentary things about him!*

Meanwhile, Misty moved restlessly. She had hoped that Alice would have come to her bed by now. It was more comfortable sleeping at night in Alice's bed than on the hard floor downstairs. Still, Alice's presence was more important to Misty than her own canine comfort, so she once again snuggled closer on the floor to Alice and returned to dreaming.

Alice was so happy to be talking and sharing her thoughts with Art, her best friend, that she was unaware he now thought of her in a much different way.

The expression "absence makes the heart grow fonder," held true for Art's feelings about Alice. He understood that Alice was more than a best friend. He respected this smart and kind, lovely young woman. Art was proud to know her, and often he discovered that there was something precious in each thought of Alice. *Am I falling in love with Alice? Would Alice ever think of me as someone she could love?*

Alice liked that Art had been listening to her explanation of the chemical research. She did not realize that Art had no particular interest in this subject, but what he did enjoy was the sound of Alice's voice, reflecting the happiness and excitement she felt as she described her discoveries.

Dawn broke. Their exhaustion became impossible to ignore. Reluctant to relinquish their pleasure in each other's company, they did realize the importance of getting some sleep. They shuffled off to their respective bedrooms to get much-needed rest...and allow Misty to nestle in bed with her mistress.

At Riverview, the next "morning" began around 12:30 p.m. for Katherine and Alice. They shared information from their recent findings. Alice thought it very clever that the Nanny-cam was disguised as a picture frame. Katherine realized why she had recognized one of the chemical names: Alice's description reminded her of Trixie's medical-treatment accident when she had been a puppy.

"Yes, now I remember that drug," Katherine replied. "When Trixie had been injured, she received a dose of this chemical. At that time, I noticed that she endured some disturbing side-effects. When I told the veterinarian about recent toxic discoveries concerning this drug, he discontinued its use on Trixie. Donald and I have long suspected that this drug may have had a connection to Trixie's advanced intelligence. Even for a Border Collie, she was extra smart."

Alice was still thinking about the Nanny-cam and asked Katherine, "Wouldn't a picture frame seem out of place in a dog's enclosure?"

"Good point. That may be true," Katherine responded, "but I've been thinking about that. If the frame was used to hold a sign, it might be accepted. It could be mounted on the back of the enclosure, facing the gate. It would then show if anyone approached the gate or if anyone was outside the enclosure watching our dog family. I'd have the sign read something like, 'Warning: Do NOT enter this area. The mother dog is very protective of her puppies!'"

"I like it!" Alice said in delight. "It would be normal and

practical to see such a sign mounted in that way. Great idea!"

By this time, Art had made his way to the kitchen, still rubbing the sleep from his eyes, when he asked, "Is there any coffee?"

The kitchen table held a basket with a few remaining muffins from breakfast. Art grabbed one as he sat at the table.

Kathrine poured her son a cup of coffee and beamed as she placed the steaming cup in front of Art. "Good morning, Sleepy-head. It actually is afternoon, you know. Did you get enough rest?" Kathrine began to fuss over her son in a motherly fashion.

Art smiled up at his mom and asked about camp. "Camp begins tomorrow; what are the plans?"

"Your father has already gone to the shelter to check on everything," Katherine answered. "Alice and I were planning to go over to the shelter soon. Misty will be able to play with her friends there, as we work on tomorrow's agenda. I believe Millie and Ruth will be there. I know it is Sunday, but we had all planned to do some work at the shelter today. Would you like to join us?"

"Yes. I really did miss not having the dog camp experience this year, but it seemed necessary for my studies. Now that I can still help, I want to. Would it be okay to ride over with you? I'm still tired and would prefer riding instead of driving. It should only take me a short time, and I'll be ready to go."

Art stuffed the muffin into his mouth and gulped his coffee. He was excited and happy that he was home and had not completely missed camp. He had almost totally forgotten about the mystery of the sick dogs.

11

SETTING A TRAP

At the Riverview Animal Shelter, the Sunday staff meeting was scheduled for 2:30 p.m.

Katherine, Alice, and Art arrived around 2 p.m. It seemed everyone wanted to welcome Art home. All were especially excited that tomorrow he would be part of the camp activities. *It's like I never left,* Art thought. *I'm NOT grateful for the problems that have been at camp, but I am grateful for the opportunity to be a part of this summer routine, once again.*

Jane was looking over the list of campers arriving the next day, Monday. The original list of those receiving the free week of camp had been shortened. A few of those eligible had previous commitments and would not be coming. A few others had stated that they were not interested in returning, even if the extra week were free.

The group gathered for their meeting, and Jane moved to the front of the room. Clearing her throat to get the group's attention, she announced, "Let me start by stating that this will not be like a regular meeting. Today I would like to have a brainstorming planning activity. I'd like this camping experience to be considered a 'sharing fun with your dog' activity.

"Every idea should be an idea for fun. I'd like activities shared with the team of camper and dog. Who wants to start?"

Ruth and Millie were the first to raise their hands. Millie presented an idea she and Ruth had been thinking about for a long time. "How about having a dog and camper obstacle course? It would be a timed challenge that could be optional for our campers to enjoy. Each session would give one team a chance to run the course twice each day. The best time would be recorded. At the end of the week, we could award the team with not only the best run-time, but they would also be required to exhibit the best attitude of encouragement to their completion.

"We have a complete proposal that we have been planning for a number of years. We thought that this might be a different fun activity we would be able to use at some point."

Jane was impressed and liked the idea. "How many of this group like this concept for a fun activity this week? Please raise your hands if you are in favor of the suggestion."

The vote was unanimous. Jane nodded to Millie and Ruth and said, "We'll use this idea beginning tomorrow. Make a copy of your plans for the group's information."

Jane then asked, "Any other ideas?"

Alice raised her hand and suggested, "I believe the Riverview Police Department has several K-9 units. I think, if I ask Detective James, we might be able to have them come and do a demonstration of their police canine work. Would you like me to look into this idea? James has said that their demonstrations are very impressive."

Again, Jane asked for a vote. A majority thought it might be good if it could be scheduled. Alice agreed to look into the possibility of a police demonstration.

It was Art's turn to raise his hand. "The Riverview beach has a section for dogs to be able to swim in the river. How about having the campers and their dogs go swimming on one of our hot days?"

Jane smiled as this idea was enthusiastically accepted.

Someone suggested a nightly campfire. Then the question of rain was raised. Jane liked the campfire idea and suggested that a "rain" option could be an indoor illusion of a campfire with possible S'more cookies or candies instead of the real thing. Once again, this new idea was welcomed.

Jane closed the session with instructions for informational hand-outs to be ready early tomorrow morning. "We'll have a brief meeting before the campers arrive. Be sure to get a good night's sleep."

Alice wanted Art to see the canine mother and her puppies, so after the meeting, she urged Art to follow her to the dogs' enclosure. Art beamed when he observed the pooches. Alice asked him, "Did you know that the puppies can't see or hear when they are born?"

Art shook his head no, but he added, "They seem to be able to see everything now."

Alice loved to watch the mother care for each puppy. "She is such a good mother!"

As Art prepared to leave, Katherine entered the area with her Nanny-cam. Creating a fib for Art's benefit, in case he wondered about this picture frame that she had been carrying, "I have brought the warning sign for this enclosure," she told Alice.

Katherine need not have said anything because Art was already lost in thought about his participation in tomorrow's events.

Smiling at their little secret, Katherine brought the Nanny-cam into the enclosure and mounted it directly across from the gate. She told Alice in a whisper, "I think it might be wise to bring Jane into our secret circle of the Nanny-cam. She could monitor this during the day, and we could take turns monitoring at night."

Alice had a question. "How can you monitor the Nanny-cam and still work at your veterinary practice?"

Katherine had already planned to take a week's vacation she told Alice. "I can take a nap during the day and be in the shelter at night. Before you ask, let me explain why I'd be at the shelter at night. If anyone gets near the enclosure, I want to be close enough to prevent any harm to our precious family."

Alice was impressed. "Yes, I can see the wisdom of bringing Jane into our secret. She is usually in her office most of the day and could easily monitor the area then. It's a good plan."

Thus, the Nanny-cam trap was set.

12

"SHARING FUN MONDAY"

Millie and Ruth had gotten up extra early to set up the obstacle course before any others at the camp could see it. They preferred to explain the various unique challenges when people had seen the course for the first time.

The **Barrel-Race** barrels were in place. Each barrel had an attachment on one side that held colored dowels. The attachments were on alternating sides. Each team would run to the side of the barrel that contained the colored dowels. They would grab a different colored dowel from each barrel, and thus they would need to run from side to side of each barrel. Every other side held the dowels. This would look similar to a horse barrel-racing competition.

The **Sawhorse Crawl** had several sawhorses with tree branches going from sawhorse to sawhorse, leaving an opening beneath the sawhorses for camper and dog to crawl under.

The **Hula-Hoop** competition involved both a throwing skill and a jumping challenge. At this location, a staff helper would give a treat to the camper. The camper was then required to put the dog into a Stay.

Then the camper had to throw the treat through the Hula Hoop and have the treat land into a metal bowl and stay there. If the treat went into the bowl but then bounced out of the bowl, the camper would be required to return to the Sawhorse Crawl and repeat this obstacle before being able to return to the Hula-Hoop challenge.

Once again, the object was to have the treat land into the bowl. If the treat landed into the bowl, then the camper would direct the dog to jump through the hoop to obtain his treat. If the dog did NOT jump through the hoop to get the treat, the camper would once again be required to return to do the sawhorse obstacle.

After completing the hoop challenge, the camper would go to a partially flattened A-frame. This was the Climbing Obstacle. Neither the dog nor the camper would be allowed to jump anywhere from the wooden frame to the ground. The exit of the A-frame was painted yellow and both dog and camper would need to step on the yellow area before they exited the A frame.

A series of **Low Jumps** completed the obstacle course. If any of the jumps had a pole knocked off as they jumped, the team would be asked to repeat the entire jump series again. This was true for both the camper and the dog. If a dog refused to jump any of the jumps, the team would also need to begin the series of jumps from the beginning. The jumps were set rather low, but this section could be a real challenge if the team had become tired.

Before anyone began the obstacle course, other teams were encouraged to watch. Emphasis was to be on their attitude of encouragement. Millie reminded the teams that the winner of the obstacle course was not only based on the shortest time but the best attitude of team encouragement as well.

The obstacle set-up had been created in a wide

circular path. On the outside of the obstacle area was an AKC (American Kennel Club) trial ring. It was a typical boundary used at many AKC functions. It did not restrict the dogs from leaving the area but did mark a boundary for the perimeter of this event. The campers had been reminded that If the dog left the ring during the run, the team would be disqualified, and they would need to wait for another turn at a future run time.

When Ben entered the camp, he began to look for Alice. He finally saw her talking to someone. *Was that Art?* Ben thought. *Isn't he staying at his college this summer and studying with a professor? What is he doing here?*

Walking toward the couple, he wanted to talk only to Alice. He planned to ignore Art. "Welcome back !" he said, directing this to Alice.

Art pretended to ignore the snub and replied, "Thanks, I'm glad to be back."

Alice realized that Ben had been referring to her, but she wanted to remind him that she had never left the camp. She had stayed to help with the clean-up. "It's good to see you, Ben. I've been participating in the camp clean-up, and you'll see a sparkling clean camp. It's going to be a fun week."

Ben felt rebuffed and annoyed at his attempt to engage Alice in conversation. He nodded to Alice to acknowledge that he had heard what she had said, but then he turned his back to her, and without saying another word, he left. *I'll go report for registration,* he thought.

Alice made a face at Art and then said something under her breath about Ben's manners. Seeing the completed obstacle course, they decided to walk in that direction.

13

MONDAY GATHERING

One by one, the campers arrived and registered. They were placed in the same cabins that they had occupied before the camp clean-up.

They noticed the obstacle set-up located on the campgrounds and wondered if something new was planned for this week.

A mandatory camper meeting was scheduled for 11.00 a.m. Lunch would be served right afterward.

The LGI was filled with excitement. Jane was pleased to see those at the meeting seemed happy, with no sign of the fear evident when they had left two weeks before.

"Welcome," Jane began. "This week's camp will be a totally different experience from anything we have ever done in the past. It will be a week of teamwork. The team will be you AND your dog. The work part will be a fun experience. My hope is that you will develop a deeper relationship with your dog during this week.

"Your first fun experience will begin this afternoon, right after lunch. Let me turn this meeting over to Miss Millie, who will explain this event."

Millie gave a brief overview of the team obstacle event.

She then said, "After lunch, get your dogs and sit on the grass outside the fenced-in ring. At that time, I will go over every obstacle and all the rules concerning each obstacle. The first run-through will NOT be timed. I'll give you a chance, instead, to get familiar with the equipment or obstacles.

"I'll emphasize something now and repeat this expectation often. Our expectation in this event is fun and sportsmanship. I will expect to see lots of encouragement for each other and I am hoping to see you having a fun time. Although there will be some competition, in this event, I want to see you enjoying the challenges of working with your dog.

"At this time, I'll turn this meeting back over to Miss Jane. She will explain our after-supper plan for even more fun."

Jane quickly began to explain the activity, "We are planning to have a campfire experience tonight. The weather is cooperating and when it is time, we will provide the ingredients for creating a S'more. If you have a joke or riddle, please plan to share it at the campfire gathering. You're dismissed for lunch."

As Ben looked over at Alice, he was pleased to see that she had not sat next to Art for the meeting. All the others were heading toward lunch, but Alice was deep in conversation with Jane. "I'm grateful for your help in this secret plan," Alice began. Then she stopped and looked around. She wondered, *had anyone been able to hear or understand what I have been saying?*

Jane nodded and simply said, "Katherine explained all of the details to me, and of course I want to help. I'm going back to my office now, and I will have a sandwich and coffee for my lunch. Now, go and join the others and enjoy your meal."

As Alice turned, Ben was standing right in front of her, wanting to sit with Alice during lunch. "It sounds like this week will be lots of fun," he said to Alice.

Alice responded, "Yes, we've come up with some good ideas. I'm looking forward to the campfire. Wait until you see the obstacle course! By the way, how was your time away from camp?"

They talked as they walked and caught up on mostly dog-related topics.

Alice told Ben about her newfound interest in chemistry. "Did you realize that there is a job with the title of Criminal Science Investigator?" Then, without waiting for an answer, she continued, "I've been doing some research on our sick-dog problem. I've discovered that some of the chemicals found here were once used for treating brain injuries. In fact, Katherine told me that her dog, Trixie, was treated briefly with one of these chemicals. She said that she felt that this was why Trixie seemed to be super-smart, even for a Border Collie."

Ben was surprised to see that Alice was interested in chemistry. He was always looking for ways to impress her. This offered him an opportunity to show off with some chemical information of his own. "Do you know that there is now one, maybe two, over-the-counter drug store products that claim to enhance the human brain's function? One of these products claims in its TV ads that it uses a substance from jellyfish."

Surprised by Ben's interest in chemistry, she asked, "You're saying that there is a manufacturer advertising that a pill will help humans improve their brain function? Wow! Guess I need to watch more TV. I didn't realize such a pill is available. I need to do some research on that product."

Alice and Ben had been scheduled for different duties

for the afternoon. Ben was going to the obstacle event and Alice was needed in the Riverview Animal Shelter.

When Alice got to the shelter, she called Detective James and asked him if the police dogs would be able to do a demonstration for the campers. James assured her that the next morning they could have one or more of the dogs attend and give a demonstration.

That Monday afternoon, Ben watched the campers navigate the obstacle challenges, learning how to become a team with their dogs. He saw that those watching the teams were also enjoying and encouraging each team's efforts.

The campers' stomachs announced mealtime was near, and the dogs indicated they needed rest, so the campers crated their dogs and moved to the food area for supper.

Art and Alice had been working that afternoon on preparations for the campfire event, with an emphasis on safety. Lots of water was available, if needed, for dousing the flames. Some fire extinguishers were positioned nearby.

"Have you ever been to a campfire?" Alice asked Art.

Art smiled as he thought of his campfire experiences. "Yes, they were so much fun. I'm hoping that ours will also be enjoyable for the campers."

Alice had never experienced a campfire. She looked forward to it.

14

THE CAMPFIRE

The sky had filled with stars.
Campers brought their flashlights, but they were not
needed around the campfire.

"Let the fun begin," Art announced. "We will begin with some riddles. I'll start. If you know the answer, feel free to yell it out. Here is the first riddle:

"What is black and white and read all over?"

"That's easy," someone shouted, "it is a newspaper."

Then that person stated another riddle:

"What is the longest word in the dictionary?

Someone yelled, "Antidisestablishmentarian."

"Wrong," the riddler replied.

Another camper announced, "It's the word 'smiles,' because it has a 'mile' between the two S letters."

This camper then asked, "Give me a bird's name that also has another bird's name within its name."

When no one could answer, Art replied. "Here is the rule. You have until tomorrow's campfire to come up with the answer. If no one can solve the riddle, that the camper who asked the riddle will give the answer and then may ask another riddle. However, if someone can answer the riddle correctly, then that person will be able to give the next riddle."

Art continued, "Now we will move on to the joke theme. Has anyone got a good joke? If possible, a good dog joke?"

One camper replied, "What is the difference between a businessman and a warm dog?"

The camper answered, "The businessman wears a suit; the dog just pants."

Another camper said, "I've got a joke: A gentleman walked into a bar one afternoon and asked, 'Does anyone here own the Pitt Bull that's tied outside?'

"Standing up, a very muscular man exclaimed, 'Yes that's my dog. What's the problem?'

"The first gentleman replied, 'I believe that my Chihuahua has just killed him.'

"'Impossible!' The Pit Bull owner announced. 'How can a little dog like yours manage to kill my big dog? What happened?'

"'Well, it seems my dog got stuck in your Pit Bull's throat.'"

Another camper offered a joke: "A man at the movie theater discovered that he had been sitting several rows behind a woman seated next to a Great Dane. He was surprised to see that this dog had been closely watching the movie. The dog would bark encouragement for the hero, growl at the bad guy, and would drool during the restaurant scenes. When the movie ended, the man walked up to the woman and asked, 'I could not help but notice that your Great Dane was closely watching the movie.'

"'Yes,' the woman agreed. 'I was surprised by his attention too. He hated the book.'"

"Here comes our guitar player. It's time now for our sing-alongs," Art announced. "There are sheets that have been handed out with the words to our songs. Each tune should be familiar to everyone."

"The first song uses the 'Happy Birthday' melody,

We're havin' fun today.
We are at camp to play.
Let us tell everybody
This campfire's fun!

"The next song will use the tune of 'Row, Row, Row Your Boat,'

Fun, fun, fun today;
Come and join our song.
Melody, melody, melody;
Voices nice and strong.
We may sing a tune
A little bit off-key.
Who will sing the best?
Certainly, all but me.

"Okay, maybe our words may not be the greatest, but let's try one last song. This will be sung to the tune of 'Take Me Out to the Ballgame,'

We must all help each other,
Encouragement every day.
With my dog and me working
And the staff leaders too,
Let me root, root, root for the others,
Fun expectations we see.
Let me play and hope for the best,
This will be my camping way.

The ingredients for the s'more fun were handed out. Each camper got a "s'more" stick. The warnings of "be careful around fire and flame" were issued, and the leaders made sure to help the campers. The dogs were in the area, but each camper made a shared effort to be extra vigilant to keep the dogs away from the campfire.

As the campfire was dying and the embers were growing cold, the campers began to return to their cabins. All seemed exhausted but happy. All were eager to crawl into their beds and get a good night's rest.

Katherine was on Nanny-cam duty this night, thankful that it had been uneventful, so far.

15

THE POLICE DEMONSTRATION

Alice stayed up late to help Art douse the campfire's hot coals. *If I stay up extra late tonight and then take a nap tomorrow afternoon, I should be able to stay up tomorrow night,* she thought.

Art was happy and full of chatter. "Did you notice how much the campers like the riddles?" Before Alice could think to answer, Art continued to talk. "Those jokes were clever, and they managed to stay with the theme of dogs. It was a good idea to ask one of the campers who can play the guitar to play the melody as we were singing. I believe the campfire was a huge success!"

Art finally took a breath and started to concentrate on his job of raking the campfire area. Alice had the watering can and used it to put out possible danger spots. She liked seeing the steam come off the hot coals and happy to let Art do the heavier raking and searching for hot spots.

It was early morning by the time their work was completed, and they retired for some much-needed sleep.

Alice set her alarm for the early morning. She wanted to greet the Police K-9 Unit and, hopefully, see James. She approached the shelter and saw Jane entering it. Alice knew that Katherine would soon be leaving to get some sleep. She hurried to catch up with Jane, just as Katherine was greeting her.

"The night was quiet, and I had all I could do to not fall asleep. It was nice to watch our canine family resting. I did notice that our mother dog continued to fuss over her puppies. She is such a good mother," Katherine reported to Jane.

"Hi, Katherine! Hi, Jane!" Alice greeted her friends. "I only got about 5 hours of sleep last night. I believe I'll be able to get a good nap this afternoon. I am excited about our Police K-9 Demo, so I'm sure I can stay awake this morning. That and I hope that I can get a hot cup of coffee."

Jane reached for the coffee pot and said, "I'm so glad this has an automatic timer. I look forward to this hot cup of coffee when I arrive in the morning!" Handing a steaming cup of coffee to Alice and then another to Katherine, Jane took her own cup and settled into her comfy office chair. "I really don't think anyone will mess with any of the dogs this morning," Jane said out loud. "The fact that there will be a large group of police coming here should enable me to plan for a quiet day." Then Jane added, "At least, I hope so."

They sat in silence for a moment. Then Alice spoke to Katherine, "I understand that you used a few tricks to stay awake. What tricks did you use to help you stay awake last night?"

Katherine had almost fallen asleep as she relaxed in one of Jane's overstuffed office chairs. Sitting up, she explained, "I knew that reading was out of the question. That would only put me to sleep. I had some word search puzzles that kept my mind alert. I had also brought some beverages high in caffeine and did a lot of walking. I'd made sure to stay too cool to be comfortable. The cold also encouraged me to want to move around. Actually, my best advice is to get a good nap in the afternoon before your shift."

Katherine gave a huge yawn and stood up. "I think it would be wise for me to go and get some sleep. I'm giving the impression that I am awake, but I'm really sleepwalking. What I need to be doing is to walk straight to a bed." Then adding, "Good night," Katherine left Jane's office.

Jane looked at Alice and could see that she was excited about the police demonstration. "Do you think that James may be coming here with the canines?" Jane asked her.

Alice, who was also hoping that he would be coming, answered, "He may not be able to come. He has a number of cases that he's been busy with. I guess I was lucky to be able to talk with him yesterday."

Alice got out of her chair and announced, "I'm too excited to sit. Do you mind if I go outside and greet the police when they arrive?"

Jane waved her hand with a "go ahead" permission. Alice almost ran out the door. Outside, she began to walk, then paced, around the shelter's front entrance. After what seemed to her an eternity, but actually was less than a half-hour, the Police K-9 Unit arrived. They were on time and ready to set up their props in the designated demonstration area.

That was when Alice learned that James would be unable to attend the demonstration. They explained that he was on another assignment. Disappointed, but having known that this was a possibility, Alice said, "I understand." Alice then directed the police unit to the area reserved for them.

Campers were arriving for breakfast. They were encouraged to eat quickly and then get their dogs. Once each got the dog, they could sit in the spectator area. The group quickly assembled.

"Welcome," the police sergeant who held the responsibility of announcer began. "We have a number of scenarios planed for our demonstration today. Please be sure to remain seated and keep your dogs close to you. There will be a certain amount of excitement and that's to be expected.

"These dogs are working dogs and they take their work seriously. To prevent any accidents, we remind you to stay seated and make sure your dog remains close by your side.

"Our first demonstration will show a search-and-rescue scenario. We have already had one of the policemen hide, and the dog was left in the police car during this time, so the dog has no idea where this man is lost. I will present something, like a piece of clothing, to our search dog. This will enable him to recognize and look for the scent of our 'lost' person.

"I'd like to show you the equipment we use to help the dog realize that he is on a search mission. This leash is a special type of leash. It enables the dog handler to give freedom to the dog but still keeps the handler close to the dog. This harness that the dog will be wearing is also made for the specific use of search and rescue. It notifies the dog and helps him do his job of searching. Watch closely and you will see how this equipment helps both dog and handler.

"Let the demonstration begin."

The K-9 handler began moving, and the campers did notice the special leash and the dog's special harness. The piece of clothing was presented to the dog for smelling. Then the dog began to search. "Please notice," the announcer said, "this dog is an air-sniffer. Some dogs are ground-sniffers. Most bloodhounds are ground-sniffers."

The dog was able to find the "lost" man in record time. As the dog kept kissing the found man, the handler pulled out the special toy reward for the police dog to enjoy playing. "Play is one of the biggest rewards for the police dog," the announcer stated. "In this scenario, the fact that someone gets found is also a major reward for the dog."

Alice was impressed with the work of this police dog. Misty was even more interested in the reward that this dog had received. *Whatever it is, this dog was really happy to receive this toy,* Misty thought.

The next scenario announced was a "bad guy" demonstration, and the announcer explained, "We will have one of the officers hold on to the 'bad guy.' This bad guy will be able to escape and run. You'll notice that we have the bad guy protected with a special bite sleeve. Our dogs do bite when they go after a bad guy. In this demonstration we don't want our human injured, so we use protective training gear. Listen to what is said when the dog is released."

The campers then saw one of the policemen holding someone. The "bad guy" struggled and started to run away. Nearby were the K-9 dog and handler. As soon as the "bad guy" began to run, the handler announced, "Stop! I'm going to release my dog and he WILL bite."

When the suspect kept running, the dog was released. As the police dog reached the suspect, he leaped at the man, who raised the bite sleeve so that the dog would bite this sleeve instead of an unprotected part of the man.

The handler then went over, gave the word for the dog to release the man, and pulled out a special toy reward for the dog.

Watching all of this, Misty was even more interested in this special toy. *Could I get that toy if I do something like this?*

"There are different dogs for different jobs," the announcer explained. "Obviously, you would not want a bomb-detection dog to act in the same way as a drug-sniffing dog.

"We will NOT be demonstrating the job of the bomb-sniffing dog, but I will tell you that this type of dog, when it recognizes the scent of a possible bomb, will simply sit and stare toward the location of the bomb. This gives the bomb unit the information it needs to be able to do something about this bomb.

"In our last demonstration, we will show you how a drug dog seeks out drugs. I'd like to reassure you that we do not use real drugs in our demonstrations. There are pseudo-drugs that we use for our training of drug dogs. These smell like the real thing but will not do the damage that a real drug could do if inhaled by our dogs.

"To answer a possible question, yes we do carry Narcan for our dogs. If our dog somehow gets some of the real drug into its system, we need to be prepared to reverse the bad effects of the drug on our dogs.

"For this demo, we have laid out a number of items that could contain drugs. There is a backpack, a cardboard box, a pair of blue jeans, and even a laundry bag. Let's see if our drug dog can find the drugs."

When the dog moved to each item and smelled each, if he did not strike an alert pose to drugs, he was told to move to the next item. The dog started to move past the back-pack then immediately returned to this item. He attacked the backpack. Scratching and attempting to open the back-pack, he managed to tear open the zipper. The special toy immediately appeared. It seemed to the dog, and everyone else, that the opening of the backpack had produced this very special and much-desired dog-toy.

Alice had to hold on tightly to Misty. Misty had once again seen the toy and was determined to investigate this special item. "No, Misty, you must stay here. Be a good girl," Alice had said.

Remembering that she had some of her own special treats for Misty, she figured this would be a good time to distract Misty with these treats. As Misty ate her treats, she kept looking at the police dog and wondering, *what do I need to do to get THAT special toy?*

The morning had been both interesting and exciting for the campers. However, it was already time for lunch. Hungry, and being discouraged from talking to the K-9 demonstration team, who were packing up to leave, the campers brought their dogs back to their crates located in the cabins. Once that was accomplished, then they traveled to the lunch area.

Alice pondered this last demo. *Misty certainly got excited during that demonstration.*

Alice walked over to her cabin. She had planned to put Misty into her crate for a rest, but she also had planned to stay at the cabin and get a few hours of sleep. Today, she had no responsibilities for the afternoon. Besides, Jane was aware of her location if anyone needed to contact her.

She pulled down the shades and closed the curtains. Then she locked the door. Closing her eyes, she wondered what would happen that evening, *will my on-guard night be quiet, or will the Nanny-cam trap capture someone?*

16

THE MAN IN BLACK

Alice had been able to get four good hours of sleep. She knew she could not be at the campfire because she would need to watch the Nanny-cam tonight. She told Art that she did not feel well and that she was going to stay in bed at her cabin instead of attending the campfire. He would also realize that she would be unable to assist in the cooling of the campfire location.

Art seemed concerned, but because he was concentrating on the campfire plans, he gave the matter little thought and told Alice, "Hope you feel better. You'll want to let Jane know that you don't feel good."

Alice smiled and thought, *that was easier than I thought it would be.* She walked to Jane's office and told her about her "cover story."

"I have one problem," Alice shared with Jane. "I want to have Misty here with me tonight. Misty and her crate are still in my cabin. How can we get them brought to this office without drawing attention to the fact that she will be at the shelter?"

"That's easy," Jane answered. "Get Misty. If anyone asks, tell them you don't feel good and I have offered to take care of her tonight, so you could get a good night's sleep. We have a number of crates here in the shelter that you would be able to use for tonight."

"That's a good idea. I'll get her now," Alice replied. "I'll lock up the cabin and leave some soft music playing so that people will think I am resting inside. Will there be some-place now that is out of the way for me to hide until you lock up for the night?"

"Alice, let me see what I can do. Get Misty and we'll work on the secret hide-a-way for you."

Alice returned with Misty. Jane secretly moved Alice into an out-of-the-way closet. No one saw the maneuver. Because there was enough light in this area, Alice felt that she could still work on some of her journaling.

"I'll let you know when I lock up everything and plan to leave," Jane told her.

A little while later, Alice could hear some of the sounds from the campfire. The answer to the riddle which asked for the name of a bird that also had another bird in its name was "meadowlark." Art had told her the answer last night as they had been working on cooling the campfire. *I never would have guessed the answer*, Alice thought.

As promised, Jane returned and said, "All clear. The shelter is locked up tight, and all is peaceful. Hopefully, your night will be a quiet one." Jane waved good-bye and walked out the front door.

Alice moved to Jane's office. Today, Alice had been glad that Jane's office had no windows to the outside grounds. Pulling out her "word search" puzzles, she began to play one of the more challenging puzzles.

Misty had fallen asleep in the office crate. Alice moved on to play a game on her cell phone. When next she looked at the time it was 3:00 a.m. The campfire had long been quiet, and Alice knew that the campers probably were in bed and asleep.

The Chemist decided to dress completely in black. Black hoodie, black sneakers, black socks, black pants, black gloves, and a black backpack. He even had a lightweight black scarf across his face. He held a tiny penlight for illumination. He had already loaded a syringe, carefully wrapped and in the front of his hoodie.

He had made sure to tape a shelter door lock to remain open, one of the back doors to the shelter. He made sure it was the one that led to the back end of the dog's area.

He would not need his backpack inside the shelter, so he decided to hide his backpack in an isolated location. *I should be able to locate that with my penlight,* he figured.

When he checked his watch, he saw that it was past 3:30 a.m. *I made sure to check all the cabins. Everyone seems to be sound asleep. The lights are dimmed at the shelter, and I'm sure that I saw everyone go home. Jane is always the last to leave. Once she left, it should be safe to enter the dog rescue area.*

Opening the taped outside door, he slowly walked toward the enclosure containing the mother and her babies. That's when he noticed and then discounted the sign, "Do not enter." *I got into the enclosure last time, and I'm sure I'll succeed again.*

The mother dog recognized that smell. She looked up and softly growled. *This is NOT a good person.* She knew he had approached her puppies before. She also remembered that the meat he had given her that last time had made her feel funny. She recalled waking up and seeing that one of her puppies had become very sick. *Something is wrong!*

Her growl grew louder.

"I've got a treat for you," the man in black said softly. He reached into his pocket and pulled out a piece of meat laced with a strong sedative. This time, the mother dog growled even louder, and she snapped at the hand that appeared with the meat.

Alice thought that she heard something. Looking at her iPhone, she saw the mother dog's enclosure. *Who is that? Someone is in the dogs' area of the shelter.* It was hard for Alice to see exactly who was pictured on the iPhone screen, but she did know that it was probably the man they were trying to catch.

Quickly locking the crate so that Mistry would not be able to follow her, Alice hurried to the inside entrance door of the dog section.

It surprised him when the mother dog lunged at his hand. He did drop the meat but noticed that the dog was not interested in eating it.

What is that noise? Alice was alarmed now.

"Who is there?" Alice yelled into the dog shelter area. Then she heard someone running.

Alice raced to the dog family's enclosure. Seeing a piece of meat on the floor inside the enclosure, she opened the gate and placed the poisoned meat outside the gate. She locked the gate, now sure that the meat would not be eaten, and she raced in the direction of the receding footsteps.

She saw the open outside door and noticed that someone had placed tape across the lock, taping it open.

Alice peered into the darkness. She was unsure if she could hear anyone still running. There was NO sign of any light in the area.

The man in black did not dare to turn on his penlight. Whoever had been in the shelter would probably see him. *I'll need to wait until morning before I pick up my backpack. It is way too dark to see that backpack without some light.* He had not figured on this.

Returning to the shelter, Alice ripped off the tape that had been on the door and then got a plastic bag for the meat. *I've probably ruined this crime scene,* she thought, *but there was no way I was going to leave that meat inside the enclosure.*

It was well after 4:30 a.m. *Should I call Jane? Should I call Katherine?* Deciding that Katherine, a veterinarian, more experienced, was the better choice, she called her first and then Jane.

"Are you OK? Did you catch the person? Did you see who it was?" Katherine asked Alice immediately after arriving at the shelter.

Alice reassured Katherine that she was fine, but the intruder had gotten away and was unrecognizable in the dark. Alice explained in detail what had taken place and then had to repeat the explanation again when Jane arrived.

Katherine checked the mother dog and her puppies, and she reported that all seemed to be healthy. "I believe you stopped a crime, but it is too bad we were unable to catch the culprit," she told Alice.

Alice was still upset and shaking. "Should I call Officer James?"

Jane suggested that they wait until it was closer to sunrise. Alice opened the door of the crate, and when Misty came out, Alice hugged Misty. As she stroked Misty's fur, Alice cried. "It is all my fault that the trap failed," she said, sobbing.

"No, it is NOT!", both women told Alice simultaneously.

Getting up from her seat, Alice announced, "I'm going back to my cabin and take a shower. Maybe then I will feel better!"

She was still holding Misty as she walked outside. The sun was just peeking over the mountains and some of the campground could be seen.

Putting Misty on the ground, Alice headed towards her cabin.

Misty was looking for a place to go to the bathroom when she saw a black lump in the distance. *What IS that? She wondered.* Going over to investigate, she became very excited. *It IS a backpack! Maybe I can get into this backpack and get that policeman's toy.* Tearing into the cloth backpack, Misty managed to rip it apart. *There is no toy? Where is the toy?*

Alice saw Misty shredding the backpack and raced to get this backpack before any more damage could occur.

Then Alice saw what Misty had caused to come out of the backpack. On the ground were syringes and vials of chemicals. *I've got to take this back to Jane and Katherine immediately.*

Disappointed, but hoping that Alice would be able to find the toy in the backpack, Misty trailed along.

"Look what I found! Actually, look at what Misty found," Alice announced as soon as she saw Jane and Katherine. "Now don't you think it's time to call James?"

17

THE BACKPACK

Alice, Katherine, and Jane searched through the backpack but found nothing to indicate to whom it belonged.

The man in black, no longer dressed in black, had decided to go out early to check the area around the shelter. *I'm sure I left the backpack near this location*, he thought. He kept searching until he saw other people appear. The camp was now awake. *I guess it would be wise to go to breakfast before someone asks me what I am looking for,* he thought.

Detective James had arrived with the Crime Scene Investigation Unit. As they looked at the contaminated crime scene, they said that they were unsure if there would be any evidence for them to recover.

"Unfortunately, your search of this backpack may make it difficult for us to analyze this bag successfully. However, we will take the backpack with us and see if there is something we can use. It is helpful that you have a copy of your observation of this man in black. We will take that with us to examine. I'll call you this afternoon if we have any information for you."

At breakfast, the suggestion was made by the staff that

today might be the perfect day to go swimming. The forecast said, "hazy, hot and humid for today. Temperatures predicted near 90 degrees Fahrenheit with a humidity level of about 70%."

Jane agreed: if they left for the beach this morning, they could also have the kitchen crew plan a picnic on the beach for their lunch. They announced that everyone should change into their bathing suits, bring their dogs, and meet at the "dogs allowed" area of the Riverview Beach.

When Alice arrived at the Riverview Beach with Misty, she noticed Art was already there. A large group of giggling girls surrounded him. Art seemed to be enjoying all the attention, and when he said something to the girls, they all laughed.

Alice looked at Misty and, disgusted, told her, "He's probably attempting to entertain them with his dumb jokes."

Then Alice looked intently at Art. It had been many years since she had seen Art with his shirt off. She admired his now-muscular body. Her girlfriends would describe their perfect man as a "hunk," and as she looked at Art, that was the word that came to her mind.

Watching the girls fuss around Art, she began to see him differently. She did not want to share her good friend with other women.

Art noticed Alice looking at him. She had a strange look on her face. But the face was not what made him stare back at her. He suddenly realized she looked great in a two-piece bathing suit. He remembered the beautiful women he had seen in a swimming sports magazine. He thought, *she looks as good, if not better, than any of the women in that magazine!*

Alice had brought Misty to the beach for play and

possible swimming. When she noticed that Art was too busy to even say hello to her, she decided that Misty would get all of her attention; she'd ignore Art.

Ben came to the beach. He had no interest in swimming and was not planning to wear a bathing suit. When he saw Art, he thought enviously, *I have no intention of parading around like Art is doing.* Ben did stare at Alice, however, hoping to get her attention.

Alice ignored both Art and Ben and was happily splashing in the water with Misty, having a grand time with throwing sticks for her dog to fetch.

Art heard it first. "Thunder! Everyone out of the water!" He yelled. "There is a storm coming. We should head back to the camp."

As they all picked up their things and started back to camp, the storm quickly overtook them.

They got soaked racing to their cabins. Once there, they grabbed towels to dry themselves and give rubdowns to their dogs. They needed to change into dry clothes.

Then out came the rain gear, and everyone headed for lunch, lots of hot chocolate and hot food. The cold rainwater had managed to cool the air and chill the campers.

At the police station, the investigators found a comb in the backpack. It did have a few hairs lodged among the comb's teeth. They wanted to check for the possibility of DNA from the hair follicles. This would need to be done in another lab.

"Is there any possibility that one of the search-and-rescue dogs might be able to get enough of a scent from this backpack and identify the rightful owner of this item?" James asked. "I think that If any dog could do this scent work, it would be Sherlock."

The K-9 team of Sherlock and his police handler held the

best reputation for any difficult tracking scenario. "We do know that it was someone in the camp. We've looked at the video. It is poor quality, but it does give us some idea of the shape of the individual who entered the shelter. I understand that the campers are indoors now, together for some activities. This would be a great opportunity to see if Sherlock can solve this case."

James was given permission to call Jane and set up a secret "smell test."

Attached to the LGI was a large storeroom. It could be accessed from an outside hall or through the LGI. The plan was to have the backpack placed in that storeroom area and when Sherlock got the scent, he would then wander into the LGI. Alice was made aware of the plan and could help in the observation of Sherlock's alert on this person.

After lunch, they set up the LGI for some games. The rain showed no sign of letting up, and the wind proved too strong to send the campers back to their cabins.

On one side, the students sat with their dogs. On the other side, the staff was seated. Alice sat with Misty at the end of the staff row, close to the storeroom entrance.

Jane was in charge of the rules for each game. She announced, "The first game will be a test of your dog's understanding of the basic positions. I will have Miss Alice and her dog, Misty, demonstrate the sequence and then each of you will get the opportunity to prove that your dog understands what you are saying."

As Alice sat in the chair, Misty had still been standing. Giving the command, "Sit," Misty immediately sat. The next command to be given was "stand." Alice stood and then said, "Stand." Misty stood. There was a towel on the floor in front of the chair. Alice lay down on the floor and then gave the command, "Down." Misty lay beside Alice on the towel. A perfect performance, three out of three, so far.

The last command was to be the command, "heel." Alice sat in the chair and had Misty sit in front of her. Then Alice said, "Heel." Misty went around the chair and to the left of Alice, heel position, and sat.

Jane explained the reasoning behind this exercise. "I'd like for you to practice giving the various words in unusual positions. If you are lying in bed and tell your dog to stand, will he know what to do?

"Each of you will now get a chance to show everyone that your dog will understand and perform as Misty has done. We'll start with the first team in the camper's row and go right down the line."

During this competition, unnoticed by anyone, Sherlock and his handler had moved into the storeroom. Actually, someone did notice. The pair had been spotted by Misty. *That is the man that gave that wonderful toy to his dog when he found the things in the backpack,* Misty thought. *Why are they here in the storeroom?*

The group had moved on to the "people and dog run-through" distraction. Half of the campers and their dogs lined up, half on each side facing the other half. There was a three-foot distance between the two lines. The dogs, standing next to their owners on each side, were placed in a sit/stay.

One camper would go to the opening of the run-through with his dog. Then he'd place the dog into a sit/stay and walk through the three-foot path toward the other open end; as he turned toward his dog, he would call his dog. The dog was expected to run down the three-foot-wide path to his person.

After completing the distraction, he would take the place of someone in the line, and that person and dog would attempt the sit/stay and then the run.

As the staff watched this distraction exercise, Misty became very interested in the fact that Sherlock's handler had a backpack in his hand. The backpack had been placed on the floor.

This dog is going to get the toy again! Misty thought. Unnoticed by Alice, Misty slipped into the storeroom and stood near the backpack.

When the backpack was opened, Misty quickly stuck her head into the opening. *I recognize that smell* she thought... *but where is the toy?* As Sherlock pushed her aside and placed his head into the backpack, Misty retreated, deciding that *maybe the toy would be given if she went to the person having the human scent of the backpack.*

Misty immediately went out and lay at Ben's feet. Ben had been sitting in the chair next to Alice, so Alice thought nothing of the fact that Misty had now moved to Ben. Sherlock followed Misty, but because of the multiple scents in the backpack, he was unsure whether to alert on Alice or Ben. Sherlock decided to sit next to Misty, between Ben and Alice.

Sherlock's handler then called the dog to him. Alice followed Sherlock and pretended that she was following Misty, as Misty had also followed Sherlock to his handler. The toy had been displayed. Misty was desperately trying to tell the handler that the toy should go to her. Sherlock was not happy to see that Misty wanted his toy.

"I think Misty wants that toy," observed Alice. Alice had managed to shut the storage room door when she entered the room. She felt a bit confused.

"Did Sherlock alert on anyone?" The handler asked.

Looking at Misty, Alice asked a question of her own. "Do you have another one of those toys?"

As the handler reached for a second toy, he began to give one toy to each of the dogs.

Alice thought for a minute and said, "Actually Sherlock sat next to Misty. That was in a location between Ben and me. So no, I do not think that Sherlock did an alert.

They walked into the hall, and Alice was disappointed in the results of this sniff test. "Did you find any other clues in this backpack?" She asked Sherlock's handler.

"Actually, we did. There was a comb with some hair in its teeth that we found at the bottom of that backpack. If we can obtain any DNA from the hair, we might be able to get an idea of a possible suspect."

"As far as any attempt to follow a scented trail from last night, I'm sure the rain has messed up any possible trail that we might have been able to follow.

"Tell Jane we will call tomorrow."

18

CLUELESS

Ben had noticed Misty when she came to lie by his feet. He thought this strange because she always stayed close to Alice, but he accepted what he felt was a compliment, and he resumed watching campers playing the distraction game.

However, after a police dog came out of the storeroom and lay down between Misty and Alice, he became disturbed by that dog's actions. When the police dog's name had been called, Sherlock got up and moved toward the caller. Misty got up and followed the police dog. Then Alice got up and followed Misty. As Alice entered the storeroom, she closed the door behind her.

What is that all about? Ben wondered.

Ben thought back to this morning and remembered that the police had come to the shelter. *Had there been a need to have them called? I'll ask Alice later.*

Just before nightfall the storm finally cleared. The campers had enjoyed playing the canine distraction games, but many had grown tired. Now that the storm was no longer a threat, it became a unanimous decision to retire early.

Katherine was scheduled to watch the Nanny-cam. *I*

don't expect to see anyone, she thought, *but it would be best to watch, just in case.*

The Chemist was troubled. *My backpack is missing, and I suspect the police now have it. I did not want to hurt those dogs. I only wanted to test my formula and make the dogs smarter. Am I in trouble? Will I be arrested for trying to do a good thing for the dogs?*

Misty was happily chewing on her toy. As Alice looked at her dog, she had the strangest feeling that she was missing something that Misty had been trying to tell her. *It WAS strange that Misty made a point of lying at Ben's feet,* Alice mused. *However, the police dog had not given a clear alert. He only sat between Misty and me.*

The next day, Thursday, would be the last full day of camp. On Friday there would only be a half-day of wrap-up activities and packing up and leaving camp.

Would that mean that this would be the end of someone's mission to hurt the dogs of the Riverview Shelter community? However, if the culprit were never caught, there would be no justice for the animals that had been hurt. The same person might hurt other dogs elsewhere.

At the police station, James was once again quizzing Sherlock's handler. "Are you sure that Sherlock did not give an alert? What exactly did Sherlock do after he smelled the backpack?"

"There was this Border Collie that came in and stuck his head into the backpack before Sherlock had a chance to sniff the article. This other dog went out and stayed by one of the camp staff." The handler told James. "After Sherlock sniffed the backpack, he went into the LGI and lay down beside that other dog. Sherlock was actually sitting between two of the chairs. Alice told me that she was sure Sherlock had not alerted on anyone."

James looked at Sherlock and jokingly gave the dog a warning. "Maybe we should consider trading you for a Bloodhound. There was a Bloodhound named 'Nick Carter,' born in the early 1900s and known for his sniffing skills. In his career, he helped identify more than 600 criminals. Should I believe that breed has a better capacity to sniff smells than you do?"

Sherlock did not reply.

With a sigh, James said to his police colleague, "Well, we still have the hairs from the comb. Have we been able to get any DNA from them?"

"Yes. They've been retrieved and tested. The DNA does not match anything in our system."

"If we were able to get DNA from the campers, would that help?" James asked.

"Remember, we cannot be sure that the comb from the backpack belongs to the owner of that backpack," James was reminded.

"Let me talk to Alice," James said. "I'm even happy with long-shot possibilities. Something would beat nothing."

19

—

BEN

—

Detective James Fields sat at his desk, staring at the phone. *I'd like to call Alice,* he thought, *and then see if we could meet at the hospital café for coffee tomorrow. This would be very short notice, but I'd like to talk to her in person. Is it too late to call her? I do have her cell phone number.*

He reached for the phone and then stopped. *I do not want to get her up if she is already asleep. Yet, I think she saw something when she watched Sherlock with the backpack and Ben but did not realize what she had seen.*

This time when he reached for the phone, he picked it up and dialed Alice's phone number.

Alice answered the phone on the second ring and recognized his voice immediately. She responded, "Oh, hi, James. What's up? Yes, I'm still awake. I just took Misty for a walk, and we're finally getting ready for bed."

James requested a coffee date for the morning and received a rapid yes. He kept the call short, deciding not to go into details about why he wanted to meet with her.

After getting off the phone, Alice looked at it as if it would give her more information. *I wonder why he wants to meet for coffee. I guess I'll find out in the morning.*

—

She climbed into bed and called Misty up to join her. After the hectic day today, she just wanted to cuddle with her dog.

The next morning, Alice got to the coffee shop before James. She'd picked up a magazine and was flipping through the pages when James arrived.

"Good morning," James said. After ordering his coffee, he got right to the subject of the coffee meeting. "I think that you did see something unusual yesterday. I understand that Misty went into the storeroom and stuck her head into the backpack. Do you know if that is true?"

"Sherlock's handler said that she had done that. I do believe him."

"What did Misty do when she came back out into the LGI?"

Alice thought for a minute and then said, "She did something unusual. She lay down by Ben's feet. I thought it was strange, but since she knows Ben, I just thought she was being friendly."

"Tell me every detail of when Sherlock came into the LGI," James urged.

"I saw Sherlock come out of the storeroom and look at Misty, then look at Ben, and then look at me, then decided to sit between Ben and myself. Looked confused," Alice added.

Interesting, James said to himself. To Alice, he added, "I have an idea, and I am hoping that maybe you can help me with it. We did recover some DNA from the comb found in the backpack. When they checked our database, they did not find a match. I know there is no guarantee that if we find a DNA match that it will prove who the backpack belongs to, but it will give us some ideas. After all, the comb could possibly be from someone other than the backpack's owner, although that seems unlikely.

"In my opinion, from what you have told me, I would suspect that Ben is the owner of the comb and the backpack."

"No!" Alice blurted out.

As the people around the coffee shop looked at Alice, James said, "Shh, please keep your voice down. You can prove me wrong if you will help me get Ben's DNA from something we are sure is his."

"Okay, I'll do it, but I think you are wrong. Ben had nothing to do with the sick puppy mystery. What do I need to do?

"Oh, I know! Ben is constantly combing his hair and losing his combs. Should I try to obtain one of those combs?"

"Good idea," James explained what was needed, and Alice agreed to obtain the hair DNA sample.

"I'll do this, and not let him catch me stealing his comb, but only because I believe this will prove that he is innocent."

Later that morning, Alice noticed that Ben was working with the campers. They were looking to improve their dog's attention around distractions.

"Hi, Ben," Alice said as she approached the group. "The dogs are paying close attention to their campers. I guess yesterday's games have made an impression."

"Yes," Ben replied, as he ran a comb through his hair, "They were impressed with the variety of ways that we tested the dog's attention. I believe they saw a value in the command of 'Watch me!'"

As the wind blew his hair once again, Ben commented, "I like my hair neat, but this wind is really messing with it today!"

One of the campers called to Ben and wanted him to look at his dog's leg. As Ben began to leave Alice, he set his comb on the bench and then moved toward the camper. With his back to Alice, she quickly grabbed the comb and turned to leave. When Ben glanced back to where Alice had been standing, he was surprised to see she was no longer there. He barely noticed his comb was gone.

Guess she was just killing time, Ben thought.

Police lab examination of the comb did produce some DNA, and James received the results later that day.

James called Alice with the results. "Alice, we got a DNA match with the hair from the comb you obtained from Ben and the hair we found on the backpack. Do you understand what that means?"

"I understand. DNA is like a fingerprint, specific to a single person."

"Yes. And since we know Ben's hair was on the comb and it matches the hair from the backpack, we know that Ben is the one who has poisoned the dogs. I know you did not want to think it was Ben, but I don't want any misunderstanding."

"No, it's clear. There's no misunderstanding on my part anymore. I understand. In fact, you can call me 'Miss Understanding.'"

"Well, Miss Understanding, without your help, we would not have solved this."

"James, that is a very generous thing to say. Thank you."

Meanwhile, Ben had grown uneasy, especially because of the reaction of the police dog. He tried to justify his actions to himself. *I am doing a good thing! Everyone should understand and realize that!* He hesitated and then decided to go to the police on his own. *I need to make them understand.*

At the police station, the clerk saw the young man enter. "Can I help you?" she asked.

"Is Detective James Fields here?" When the clerk nodded yes, the young man said, "Could I see him, please?"

James walked into the lobby, saw who was there, and

directed him to one of the interview rooms. "Ben, it is nice to see you. Why did you want to see me?"

That was when Ben confessed to what he had done to the dogs. He explained his reasons and that he really was trying to improve the lives of the dogs.

After some legal formalities, James arrested him and explained that he would get a chance to tell his story to a judge.

James called the shelter and told Jane what had happened.

At the Riverview Animal Shelter, Katherine, and Jane were shocked to hear Ben was responsible for the sick dogs. Soft-hearted Jane felt that although Ben had definitely experimented the wrong way, he was attempting to do something good.

Jane said, "Ruth, one of my CEOs used to say that it is not a bad thing if you learn from it. I'm thinking that if we can be sure that Ben will never attempt to experiment on a dog in the future, maybe we should recommend probation and community work instead of jail time."

20

COLLEGE PLANS

Ben stood before the judge, nervous and unsure of what to expect.

Judge Thomas looked at the paperwork in front of him and then at Ben. "I see that you have never been arrested, nor, as far as I can see, ever even received a traffic ticket. You've been a good, upstanding citizen all of your life."

Looking once again down from the bench, he continued, "That is why the prosecution's recommendation for no jail time makes good sense to me. I will sentence you to five years of probation and 1,000 hours of community service. Your community service will be with the Riverview Park Service. You will report to their supervisor first thing on Monday morning."

Ben may have been a free man, but he was all alone.

No one from the Riverview Animal Shelter had attended this court session. Ben's family had made no attempt to contact him, nor did they attempt to come to Riverview.

As Ben stepped out from the courthouse onto the sidewalk, he turned in the direction of Riverview Park.

What was in Ben's future? Could Ben ever work with animals again?

Lots of questions but no real answers

He was last seen walking toward the river. Where did he go?

In another section of Riverview, Art had been sitting at the breakfast table with his mom and dad.

Art was saying, "As you know, I've been accepted at Mom's veterinarian college. I plan on following in Mom's footsteps and becoming a veterinarian. I'll be transferring my college credits from Buffalo there.

"Dad, I was wondering, Mom was able to use your condominium apartment in New York City. Is there any chance I could use that same apartment while I'm at college?"

Don smiled and said, "I don't see why not. I'll look into it for you. When will you begin your schoolwork?"

Art replied pleasantly, "It will not be for a few weeks. Alice and I plan to help at the shelter. She will also be doing some shadowing at the CSI lab at the Riverview Police Station.

"Did I tell you that she found a college in New York City that offers Forensic Science? She wanted me to ask you if your contact at the condominium knows of any units or reasonably priced places to rent," Art added.

Donald answered, "I'm not sure but I will look into it for her. I know they had some efficiency rental apartments. Does she plan on having Misty live there with her?"

"Oh yes, I forgot to mention that. Will that be a problem?" Art asked. "She said she would feel safer if she had Misty with her."

Donald just nodded and assured Art that he would look into this for Alice as well.

Alice was grateful that James somehow had managed a "shadowing" opportunity for her at the CSI. He could only arrange for a few weeks, but Alice welcomed the chance to see this lab in action.

Between helping at the shelter and the time at the CSI lab, Alice barely had enough time to pack for college.

Alice was invited to Art's home for dinner about one week before they would be leaving for college. At that time, Alice made a point of personally thanking Donald for arranging a reasonably priced efficiency apartment for her and for arranging that she could also have Misty with her.

Donald assured her that the connections he had with his real estate friend made many impossible things possible.

Art and Alice received their college class schedules. When they compared their class times, Art realized that all his classes were in the morning and Alice realized that all her classes were in the afternoon.

"I can watch Misty for you while you are in class." Art announced.

"Thank you; that is awesome. I was worried about Misty during the times I would be away from the apartment." Alice laughed and gave a sigh of relief.

James and Alice saw very little of each other. They may have worked in the same building but between the crazy hours and the places that they needed to go, it was almost impossible for them to connect. Just before Alice had to leave for college, they made a coffee date appointment.

"I'll be leaving for college in a few days," Alice told James.

"Yes, I knew you would be leaving soon. When is your first break from college?"

"James, I'm not sure. The first big break will not be until Christmas. Want to plan a Saturday that we might be able to meet for dinner?" Alice wanted to make sure that she would be able to see him before the new year.

"How about the Saturday after Thanksgiving. It should work," James suggested.

"Let's plan for then, and if I don't see you before I go,

take care of yourself," Alice said as she stood up to go. They hugged and once again traveled in different directions.

The day of moving to New York City began with Donald and Art loading Donald's truck and Art's car. Alice was to meet them at the NYC apartment building. Conveniently, her efficiency apartment and his condo were located in the same building. Art had already picked up a few of Alice's pieces of furniture and promised to help get those pieces to her apartment.

As is often the case in romance stories, the weather did co-operate the day Alice and James were to meet.

ABOUT THE AUTHOR

Helen Bemis has enjoyed working with dogs all her life.

She is grateful for the opportunity to help others understand these loving companions, as she endeavors to enrich the human-dog bond through tools of love.

She grew up on a dairy farm in Upper New York State; after graduating high school, she attended Albany Medical Center School of Nursing. She is married and has three children.

She obtained a college degree at SUNY Adirondack, earned the Certified Professional Dog Trainer international certification and has a successful business, K-9 Karing. She has been a Therapy Dog evaluator and is an A. K. C. award evaluator. She has judged fun dog matches, often speaks to many organizations and teaches dog safety and other dog-related topics to schools as well as at her local college.

This is her sixth Riverview Animal Shelter book, the first five being *Understanding Sassie; Understanding Sassie,*

II; Understanding Champ; Understanding Trixie, and *Understanding Tippie.*

She loves to hear people say, "Helen has gone to the dogs."

Contact Helen via:
K-9 Karing, LLC
Helen Bemis, CPDT-KA
P.O. Box 67
Ganesvoort, NY 12831-0067
Phone: 518.584.5357
Email: K9KaringHelen@nycap.rr.com

ABOUT THE ARTIST

MECHELLE ROSKIEWICZ
29 Fourth Avenue, Warrensburg, NY 12885
Cell phone: 518-744-7911
loveddogsart@gmail.com, loveddogsart.com

Creating animal-inspired art and one-of-a-kind portraits in painting and sculpture, artist Mechelle Roskiewicz captures their loving spirit and beauty. She has commissions throughout the United States and the world, including paintings in the Kennel Club of England's Library, CEO's Office and their prestigious Art Room in London. Published in magazines, books and producing illustrations, she continues to explore and expand her passion for art.

Mechelle lives in Warrensburg, NY, with her husband, James, and her two muses, Lilly and Ella, both Cavalier King Charles Spaniels.

REVIEW THIS BOOK?

Authors and their readers rely heavily on reviewers to help them find each other. Please help by writing a review wherever you wish.

Amazon.com sells more than half the books sold in the US; to review this book there, find *She is Miss Understanding* in their Books category and click on the button "Write a customer review." It will be appreciated by the author and her potential readers.

Lightning Source UK Ltd.
Milton Keynes UK
UKHW021419030720
365983UK00004B/483